D1156703

WILLIAM FAULKNER: *New Orleans Sketches*

WILLIAM FAULKNER

New Orleans Sketches

INTRODUCTION BY CARVEL COLLINS

Rutgers University Press, NEW BRUNSWICK, N. J.

1958

The publisher wishes to thank William Spratling
for the use of the sketch of William Faulkner
on which the title-page drawing is based.

First printing

Contents

Contents

About the Sketches

IN 1925 AT THE AGE OF twenty-seven William Faulkner, who had been up to then almost exclusively a poet, began to publish fiction. During that year, in which he lived for six months at New Orleans, he contributed sixteen signed stories and sketches to the Sunday feature section of the New Orleans *Times-Picayune*. These pieces are of interest; so I was delighted, exactly a quarter-century after their publication, to come upon them in the *Picayune* files—and grateful to Mr. George W. Healy, Jr., Managing Editor of the *Times-Picayune*, for at once giving permission to reproduce them.

But before they could be reproduced the staff of *Faulkner Studies*, having learned of the existence of eleven of the sixteen sketches, reprinted those in 1953 as *Mirrors of Chartres Street by William Faulkner*. In 1955, after two additional *Picayune* sketches of the "Mirrors" type had been brought to their attention, the same editors reproduced them in a volume called *Jealousy and Episode: Two Stories by William Faulkner,* thus bringing back into print in two volumes thirteen of the sketches. Those reprintings still left three long, signed stories by Faulkner buried in the 1925 file of the *Picayune,* and the reprints contained many misreadings, omissions, and additions. So it seems useful now to put together all sixteen sketches as one volume with a more accurate text. In addition, the present volume reprints "New Orleans," a group of short sketches which Faulkner published in the January–February, 1925, issue of the New Orleans literary magazine, *The Double Dealer.*

William Faulkner had ended one phase of his life when he reached New Orleans in 1925. Three years before, he had come home from New York to act as temporary postmaster at the University of Mississippi; and to take an examination for the permanent postmastership on December 3, 1921. The next spring he had become permanent postmaster and had held the position until he resigned on October 31, 1924. The experience was not pleasant, and immediately after his resignation he made his now famous remark about the relief of being no longer at the beck and call of everyone who, in that day of cheaper postage, had two cents. He also seemed glad to be free to give full time to writing—free, as he told a friend the day after his resignation, to be outdoors watching the color of life, to take pipe and paper, and to dream and write. He added in his comments to this friend that he no longer intended to be controlled by the clock or by the daily routine of conventional employment.

Another friend, Phil Stone, remembers that Faulkner had gone to New York before the post-office job not only to study graphic arts but to be nearer publishers, who might accept his poetry. Now, with the postmastership ended, he apparently decided to go to Europe, acting perhaps, as Phil Stone suggests, on the principle that one good way to get literary recognition in the United States is to get it abroad, a principle which had already served Robert Frost— and was later to serve Faulkner in ways no one could then foresee.

He may also have decided to join other exiles in Europe in reaction against the state of literary life in America, for he spoke sharply of this in an essay published by the New Orleans *Double Dealer* almost as soon as he reached the city:

The American critic . . . takes the piece under examination for an instrument upon which to run difficult arpeggios of cleverness. This seems so sophomoric, so useless . . .

How much better they do this sort of thing in England than in America! Of course there are in America critics as sane and tolerant and as soundly equipped, but with a few exceptions they have no status: the magazines which set the standard ignore them; or finding conditions unbearable, they ignore the magazines and live abroad. In a recent number of "The Saturday Review" Mr. Gerald

Gould, reviewing "The Hidden Player" by Alfred Noyes, says:

"People do not talk like that . . . It will not do to set down ordinary speech of ordinary people; that would generally be dull . . . To give the deadly detail is misleading." Here is the essential of criticism. So just and clear and complete: there is nothing more to be said. A criticism which not only the public, but the author as well, may read with profit. But what American critic would let it go at this? . . . The English review criticizes the book, the American the author. The American critic foists upon the reading public a distorted buffoon within whose shadow the titles of sundry uncut volumes vaguely lurk. Surely, if there are two professions in which there should be no professional jealousy, they are prostitution and literature.

Whatever his reasons, Faulkner seems to have made clear as he left Oxford that he was leaving the country, for the author of a "Hayseed Letter" in the University of Mississippi student newspaper for December 5, 1924, said that Faulkner had "done give up the post offise . . . It is rumored that Bill will retire to some tropic iland, lay in the sweet smelling locust leaves and gourd vines and indite sonnets to the pore helpless world, which no one can diagnose." The town newspaper more soberly said, "Reports are current that Mr. Falkner will go abroad in the near future." Additional evidence against the occasionally expressed opinion that Faulkner went to New Orleans to settle in the literary group around Sherwood Anderson is in John McClure's review of *The Marble Faun*, written for the *Picayune* almost as soon as Faulkner reached New Orleans: "This reviewer believes that Mr. Faulkner promises fine things. He is soon off for Europe."

But Faulkner postponed his embarkation, settled in the Vieux Carré, and began almost at once to write the sketches and stories which are reprinted here. Previously he had published two pieces of fiction—a story and a short sketch, both in the University of Mississippi student newspaper. He had tried his hand at drama in at least one unpublished college play and in *Marionettes*, which he "published" himself during 1920, hand-lettering the booklets, skillfully illustrating them after the manner of Beardsley, and giving them to a few friends. He had also written a large quantity of poetry, from which he had published one poem in *The New Republic* (1919), one in *The Double Dealer* (1922), and many in the University of Mississippi yearbook and newspaper. He had prepared a volume of poems, then called *The Greening Bough*, which was to appear a decade later, and had just brought out, late in 1924, his first book of poems, *The Marble Faun*, with an introduction by Phil Stone.

Though he must have felt some disappointment because his poetry was not being more widely published, he kept his sense of humor: when *The New Republic*, which had accepted "L'Apres-Midi d'un Faune," returned other poems, Faulkner and Stone as a joke submitted a poem by John Clare without identifying its author. After it was rejected, they submitted "Kubla Khan." They were amused when the editor, in returning this poem also, said that he liked it, Mr. Coleridge, but it didn't seem to be getting anywhere.

Faulkner's poetry, published and unpublished, and his early critical essays show how much he had been interested in the work of, among others, Shelley, Keats, Verlaine, Housman, Eliot, Pound—and Swinburne, whom he called, in a review for the college newspaper, "a mixture of passionate adoration of beauty and as passionate despair and disgust with its manifestations and accessories in the human race." Other reviews he wrote for the college paper showed his admiration for Conrad Aiken—a "rift of heaven sent blue"—as well as his disapproval of poetry by Vachel Lindsay and Carl Sandburg. Of Amy Lowell he wrote in 1921 that she "tried a polyphonic prose which, in spite of the fact that she had created some delightful statuettes of perfectly blown glass, is merely a literary flatulency; and it has left her, reed in hand, staring in naive surprise at the air whence her bubbles have burst."

Through the publication by *The Double Dealer* of his poem "Portrait" (1922), William Faulkner had made his first connection with New Orleans' literary life. When he reached New Orleans in 1925 he found that the magazine's office, in an old building at 204 Baronne Street, was one of the focal points for the literary people of the city. And he found in one of its editors a man who would be an active sponsor and close friend for many years: John McClure, whose remarkably perceptive reviews were a feature of *The Double Dealer* and whose regular column in the *Picayune*, "Literature—and Less," made its Sunday issues outstanding among American newspapers which published book pages. McClure, Julius Friend, Albert Goldstein, and Basil Thompson had founded *The Double Dealer*, in January, 1921. Soon its Managing Editor was Lillian Friend Marcus, who has kindly given permission to republish in this volume Faulkner's "New Orleans." Among the magazine's authors were Sherwood Anderson, Hart Crane, John Crowe Ransom, Djuna Barnes, Robert Penn Warren, Maxwell Bodenheim, Carl Van Vechten, Hamilton Basso, Donald Davidson, James Feibleman, Mark Van Doren, Ezra Pound, Malcolm Cowley, Howard Mumford Jones, Thornton Wilder, Allen Tate, and Edmund Wilson. A point of justifiable pride with the former editors and publishers of *The Double Dealer* is that they printed the work of both Hemingway and Faulkner—so early, in fact, that when a sketch by Hemingway appeared in May, 1922, the magazine's notes on contributors said of him, "Ernest M. Hemingway is a young American writer who lives in Paris and enjoys the favor of Ezra Pound. He expects shortly to bring out a book of poems."

One of *The Double Dealer* founders, Albert Goldstein, remembering that the magazine had been intended not only to encourage new writers but to prove to H. L. Mencken the error of his contention that the

South was without culture, has pointed out that it accomplished both missions, for in its six years of existence it not only established an admirable list of "firsts" among authors but impressed Mencken enough for him to write in *The Smart Set* that *The Double Dealer* was delivering the South from a cultural swamp.

Examination of *The Double Dealer* quickly makes clear that the people who ran it—with whom William Faulkner associated in these months of 1925 and when he returned to New Orleans in 1926—were fully aware of the intellectual and aesthetic currents which were making the twenties so important in American literature. And with our knowledge of Faulkner's subsequent writing it is pleasant to read the prophetic editorial by Basil Thompson, first published in 1921 and republished in a memorial issue in 1924, which said, almost as though Mr. Thompson could foresee Faulkner's career:

It is high time, we believe, for some doughty, clear visioned penman to emerge from the sodden marshes of Southern literature. . . .

It is no idle conceit to hazard that some Southern Sherwood Anderson, some less tedious Sinclair Lewis, lurks even now in our midst. . . . There are hundreds of little towns in Alabama, Mississippi and Louisiana fairly bubbling with the stuff of stories. . . . The old Southern pot-boiler must go out—the lynching-bee, little Eva, Kentucky Colonel, beautiful Quadroon stuff—a surer, saner more virile, less sentimental literature must come in. By all the symptoms the reaction is near at hand.

Sherwood Anderson was clearly the greatest celebrity in what Faulkner has since called "our small New Orleans group." Early in 1922 Anderson had lived briefly in New Orleans, taking a room in the French Quarter and reporting that he had come to New Orleans "because I love something basically cultural in the life here, because there is published in this city the *Double Dealer*." He went on in the same magazine article to urge other artists to come to New Orleans:

. . . I address these fellows. I want to tell them of long quiet walks to be taken on the levee in back-of-town, where old ships, retired from service, thrust their masts up into the evening sky. On the streets here the crowds have a more leisurely stride . . . I stick to my pronouncement that culture means first of all the enjoyment of life, leisure and a sense of leisure. It means time for a play of the imagination over the facts of life, it means time and vitality to be serious about really serious things and a background of joy in life in which to refresh the tired spirits.

In a civilization where the fact becomes dominant, submerging the imaginative life, you will have what is dominant in the cities of Pittsburg and Chicago today.

When the fact is made secondary to the desire to live, to love, and to understand life, it may be that we will have in more American cities a charm of place such as one finds in the older parts of New Orleans now.

In the summer of 1924, after he had married Elizabeth Prall, Anderson returned to New Orleans, settling with a feeling of permanence in the Quarter.

Faulkner apparently visited New Orleans in late 1924, perhaps primarily to meet Anderson. The meeting must have been easier because of Faulkner's previous acquaintance with Mrs. Anderson, whom he had known in New York when he worked for her in a bookshop. According to one friend he had become eager to meet Anderson as soon as he had read *Horses and Men*, which Anderson published in 1923; and on the way to New Orleans Faulkner told that friend he ranked "I'm a Fool" with Conrad's *Heart of Darkness*: the two finest stories he had ever read.

Faulkner apparently at once impressed Anderson —if one assumes that the piece called "A Meeting South," which Anderson said he wrote in 1924 and which he published in April, 1925, is partially based on their first meeting. And Faulkner was impressed, as he soon pointed out in a Texas newspaper article, by Anderson's indigenous quality, his being an "American, and more than that, a middle westerner of the soil . . . A field of corn with a story to tell and a tongue to tell it with." When Anderson returned to New Orleans in March, 1925, after a two-months lecture tour, the two men spent a great deal of time together, sauntering in the Quarter and along the Mississippi, and sitting at cafes and in Jackson Park. Once, according to Faulkner, they took a brief trip on a river boat, and they joined in yachting excursions on Lake Pontchartrain which were to contribute to Faulkner's novel *Mosquitoes*, in which Anderson would appear as Dawson Fairchild.

Both men later reported that their association had turned Faulkner toward fiction, and that it was Anderson who had placed Faulkner's first novel, *Soldiers' Pay*, with Boni & Liveright. In 1929 Faulkner dedicated his novel *Sartoris* "TO SHERWOOD ANDERSON *through whose kindness I was first published, with the belief that this book will give him no reason to regret that fact.*"

After 1926 Anderson resented the parody of him by Hemingway in *Torrents of Spring* and the milder parody by Faulkner in the introduction to *Sherwood Anderson & Other Famous Creoles*. But in spite of his reaction to the parody, Anderson throughout his life showed no signs at all of regretting his early sponsorship of Faulkner's writing: he told Liveright that Faulkner had a good future; he wrote Maxwell Perkins that stories by Hemingway and Faulkner gave him "a grand thrill"; he told his friend Roger Sergel that Faulkner and Hemingway had not "sold out their imaginative life"; he wrote in 1935 that "Stark Young and his sort ignore" the "beaten, ignorant, Bible-ridden, white South" of Huey Long but that "Faulkner occasionally really touches it"; in the same year he listed Faulkner and Hemingway among professional writers who properly knew themselves to be "real" writers; and in 1937 he wrote that Faulkner, like Wolfe, "may write of terrible happenings, but you feel always an inner sympathy with the facts of life itself."

Faulkner has said that what he calls "the unhappy

caricature affair" of *Sherwood Anderson & Other Famous Creoles* led Anderson to decline to see him for years. They apparently met only a few more times: at a cocktail party in New York, when Faulkner realized once more than Anderson was "a giant in an earth populated to a great—too great—extent by pygmies," and at a brief writers' conference in Virginia during 1931 when they must have had little communication in the large crowd, where the other celebrities ranged from Ellen Glasgow, James Branch Cabell, and John Peale Bishop to the author of *Mrs. Wiggs of the Cabbage Patch.* In 1937, while the Algonquin was still a center for artistic people in New York, they met there a time or two. In 1940, not long before he died, Anderson wrote for the Gotham Book Mart's *We Moderns* a brief account of his association with Faulkner in New Orleans, and praised more than his fiction, saying that Faulkner was a "story teller but he was something else too. The man is what they mean in the South when they use the word 'gentle.' He is always that. Life may be at times infinitely vulgar. Bill never is."

Sherwood Anderson & Other Famous Creoles, with its skillful parody by Faulkner of Anderson's warm, folksy, sometimes bumbling style, was the product of a collaboration between Faulkner and the artist William Spratling, who is mentioned several times in the *Picayune* sketches which are being reprinted here. Spratling was then a teacher of architecture at Tulane University, and now lives in Taxco, where he is responsible for the revival of native crafts. He lived on an upper floor of the building in which Faulkner rented a ground-floor room during most of his 1925 sojourn in the Quarter—at Number 624 in Orleans Alley, the picturesque street running along the pleasant open grounds at the rear of St. Louis Cathedral and now called "Pirates' Alley" for the tourist trade. Spratling recalls—as does Mrs. John McClure, who lived on another floor of the same building—that it was customary to find Faulkner writing full-blast from very early morning. In the *Picayune* sketch called "Out of Nazareth," Faulkner names Spratling as his companion on a walk in the Quarter and refers to him as one "whose hand has been shaped to a brush as mine has (alas!) not." Faulkner had long been interested in drawing and painting and had shown real skill in the sketches for his play *Mario-nettes* and in the many drawings he had made for the University of Mississippi yearbook and for a humor magazine; and a fine sense of color in the paintings which illustrate his unpublished *Mayday*. But Faulkner no longer had aspirations to be a professional graphic artist: in "Out of Nazareth" he wrote not only that Spratling's hand was "shaped to a brush," but that for himself "words are my meat and bread and drink." To pool these talents, Spratling and Faulkner collaborated on *Sherwood Anderson & Other Famous Creoles* in 1926. The previous year Miguel Covarrubias had published *The Prince of Wales and Other Famous Americans*, a book of caricatures of American celebrities. *"With Respectful Deference To* MIGUEL COVARRUBIAS," Spratling drew for *Sherwood Anderson & Other Famous Creoles* cartoon portraits of forty-one members of the artistic and literary circles of New Orleans, beginning with Sherwood Anderson and including Roark Bradford, then an editor of the *Picayune;* John McClure; Lillian Marcus, sketched as though for an illustration on the cover of *The Double Dealer;* Hamilton Basso, then studying at Tulane; and Lyle Saxon. The book ended with a caricature of Spratling and Faulkner, well supplied by three jugs, drawing and writing under a wall sign proclaiming "Viva Art." They dedicated the volume "To ALL THE ARTFUL AND CRAFTY ONES OF THE FRENCH QUARTER." Spratling remembers that they "unloaded 400 copies on friends at $1.50."

One of the most colorful among the friends who probably bought this book was a man who is said to have intrigued Faulkner in those New Orleans months: Colonel Charles Glenn Collins. He was a Scot whose conversational skill and candor made days at Lake Pontchartrain, in boats or on the beaches, pleasant for Faulkner and the rest of the group. His had been a life of adventurous ups and downs, as his manuscript autobiography, kindly lent me by his family, clearly shows. Its most noteworthy feature as far as New Orleans was concerned had ended not long before Faulkner reached the city: because of the Colonel's alleged failure to pay for $50,000 worth of jewelry in Bombay, he was held for a time in jail at New Orleans while he made what the New Orleans *Item* reported to be the longest fight against extradition in American history. According to local rumor his incarceration had one charming feature: his jailers regarded him so highly that he could charter a yacht from time to time and cruise about Lake Pontchartrain entertaining the jailers and his literary and artistic friends. Early in 1924 he was completely freed of the charges and returned to life in the Quarter. The Colonel seems to have furnished the basis for a character in *Mosquitoes*—as did several other members of the Quarter's literary group.

It is possible that a few suggestions for the character in *Mosquitoes* named Pete, or for his older brother, Joe, and more suggestions for a character in the *Picayune* sketch "Country Mice," reprinted here for the first time, came from the life of a man called "Slim," an adjunct of the artistic circles of the Quarter during Prohibition. As the New Orleans *Item* recalled at the time of "Slim's" murder in 1937, "His associations with liquor establishments in the Vieux Carre made him one of the best known men in that section, it was said." He was a man who commanded attention —and William Faulkner's interest. One former reporter for the *Picayune* remembers that some of the young men on the staff banked their money with "Slim," who would dole it out to them in small, regular amounts to help budget their expenditures, for no one would have thought of arguing with him. He had studied for the priesthood, was well read, ran his business affairs smoothly, and kept out of the papers during his active professional career. He is said to have used many boats in his business; and possibly it was with him that Faulkner, in the episodes he has spoken about, would go across the Lake into the Gulf and lie-to without lights until the Coast Guard patrols had passed.

Roark Bradford, one year older than Faulkner, was another of his New Orleans acquaintances. Bradford admired him as a man and as an artist. A few years later, when Faulkner had published important novels, Bradford told New Orleans friends that he considered him the greatest American writer. They spent many leisure hours together, often shared with their mutual friend, John McClure. One of their favorite spots was a table in the corner of a cabaret in Franklin Street just off Canal, where the music of the talented clarinetist, Georgia Boy, especially delighted Faulkner. Another cafe where these friends spent some of their time was one which the owner is said to to have used as his business headquarters in directing much of the section's most lucrative commercial activity, but which he ran with decorum—and considerable style, serving the best Roquefort sandwiches John McClure remembered ever having tasted. H. L. Mencken, who was an admirer of McClure's poetry and criticism and who continually urged him to publish more, sometimes visited New Orleans. On these occasions Faulkner is reported to have let the others do most of the talking—as he did when he was with his friends at the *Picayune* offices, according to one of the former reporters, Mr. George Tichenor, who recalls that all the younger men "looked up to stars of real magnitude on the city staff. There were at the time Roark Bradford, John McClure, Lyle Saxon, Gwen Bristow, a little Englishman named Eddie Dix, who turned out to be a Lord incognito, and several assorted crackpots of dash and ability. Dorothy Dix was retired but chummy." Mr. Tichenor remembers that the *Picayune* had a predilection for hiring military men, one of them being the Managing Editor, Colonel James Edmonds, who took a liking to Faulkner and must have favored the idea of his publishing a series of sketches in the paper.

The sketches, which began appearing in the *Picayune* on February 8, 1925, were probably paid for at the going rate of between fifteen and twenty-five dollars for a half-page of the Sunday feature section. It is frequently said that Sherwood Anderson stimulated Faulkner to write fiction, and Faulkner himself generously supports this view; but it is doubtful that the earliest among these sketches and stories in the *Picayune* and the sketches which appeared in the first issue of *The Double Dealer* for 1925 were the product of Sherwood Anderson's daily example as a writer, because Anderson was away from New Orleans during January and February of that year. But however they were inspired, these sketches and stories foreshadowed much of Faulkner's mature subsequent work. As the series progressed through 1925 Faulkner moved closer to his later subjects, near the end even taking up one element of his characteristic subject matter by setting "The Liar" in the back country far removed from New Orleans, the Vieux Carré, and Chartres Street.

In selecting "Mirrors of Chartres Street" as the title for his first sketch and as the subtitle for most of his other *Picayune* pieces, Faulkner was surely being ironical. The *Picayune* carried a "Mirrors of Washington" column full of accounts of men of national affairs; and Harold Begbie's *Mirrors of Downing Street* was extremely popular just then, with its descriptions of men in the highest echelons of British government. Faulkner's "Mirrors"—held up to a main thoroughfare in the French Quarter—reflect entirely different people: the protagonist of the first sketch is a crippled beggar, and the series goes on to include as central characters a dynamiter, race-track touts, a pathologically jealous restaurant owner, a jockey, bootleggers, an aged cobbler, and a youthful hoodlum. Instead of being men of power and substance, many of the characters in Faulkner's "Mirrors" are alien, either to American life, like the narrator in "The Cobbler," or to city life, like the confused and victimized up-country Negro in "Sunset." The author shows his respect and sympathy for these people, in the first sketch of the series praising the "untrammelled spirit" of the crippled beggar and likening him to "Caesar mounting his chariot among cast roses."

Faulkner perceives their hunger—for recognition, for love, for status, for dignity—and makes it a major theme of these sketches.

Just as Faulkner expanded the themes of some of the short "New Orleans" sketches of *The Double Dealer* into the *Picayune's* longer pieces, among them "The Cobbler" and "Frankie and Johnny," so he was to enlarge and enrich in great novels many of his themes from the *Picayune*. The reference in "Out of Nazareth" to the calm belief of a pregnant woman that nature will care for her anticipates Lena Grove of seven years later in *Light in August;* the same sketch, with its comment that the men in the park "had learned that living is not only not passionate or joyous, but is not even especially sorrowful," anticipates in a small way the attitude Mr. Compson was to express to his son Quentin in *The Sound and the Fury;* the musical saw of "Home" was to reappear, put to more symbolic use, in *The Sound and the Fury;* in "The Kingdom of God" the cornflower blue eyes of the idiot, his broken narcissus, his bellowing, and his silent departure from the final furious scene, anticipate the extended and effective treatment of Benjy in *The Sound and the Fury;* the horse which runs through Mis' Harmon's house in "The Liar" was to grow into the horse which invades Mrs. Littlejohn's house in *The Hamlet*, in fact into the whole wild herd of spotted horses; in the same sketch the store, which would have to be changed only by the addition of the monstrous Flem Snopes to become Will Varner's place

27

at Frenchman's Bend, also anticipates *The Hamlet;*
"Yo Ho and Two Bottles of Rum," until now buried
like "The Liar" and "Country Mice" in the *Picayune*
files, points ahead to one of the more startling aspects
of *As I Lay Dying,* as the corpse of the too-long-dead
Chinese cabin boy is carted under the blazing sun.

Large motifs are foreshadowed here also. In his
novels Faulkner was to make much use of parallels
with Christian belief and ritual, notably in *Sartoris,
The Sound and the Fury, As I Lay Dying, Light in
August, Pylon, The Hamlet,* and *A Fable.* In small
ways these sketches anticipate that characteristic
practice. For example, "Out of Nazareth" hints, by
more than its title, at a parallel with Christ. Its central character is a youth, innocent and loving and
friendly to the humble of the earth, who has slept in
hay among cattle, who is "eternal." Having "served
his appointed end" so that he "now need only wait,"
he is staring at the spire—the cross?—of the Cathedral "or perhaps it was something in the sky he was
watching." He is on the point of departure, and he
leaves a message of good cheer. He is not specifically
equated to Christ, but he is called David, who is
pointed out by the New Testament and by official
religious publications to have been "both a prophet
and a type of Jesus Christ." And in light of
Faulkner's later practice, the characteristics and experiences of the David in "Out of Nazareth" suggest
Christ's, a possibility increased by the fact that this
sketch was published in the *Picayune* on Easter Sun-

day, 1925, and was not labeled as part of the "Mirrors of Chartres Street" series despite its setting in the Quarter.

Another motif associated with an important religious figure which Faulkner was to expand beyond its appearance in the *Picayune* concerns Saint Francis of Assisi. The *Picayune* sketch "The Kid Learns" ends when the young gangster confronts a girl, "all shining and her hair that wasn't brown and wasn't gold and her eyes the color of sleep," and learns as he dies that she is "Little sister Death." This use of the addition which the dying Saint Francis made to his "Canticle of Creatures" was to reappear in Faulkner's work. In a general way it seems already to have been in his poem "The Lilacs," published in *The Double Dealer* in June, 1925, but written much earlier. More significant use of it is in the later, unpublished work titled *Mayday*: When Sir Galwyn of Arthgyl, rid of Hunger, the companion who has been on his right hand, and of Pain, the companion who has been on his left hand, approaches his end at the stream, he sees Saint Francis and gladly joins the shining maiden who he learns is Little Sister Death. A published later use of this motif, more elaborate because of problems about the protagonist's real sister, was to be in *The Sound and the Fury* when Quentin Compson, also accompanied by a kind of hunger and a kind of pain, brooding on Saint Francis who had "said Little Sister Death," thinks of his own approaching death at the river.

Elements of Faulkner's later techniques are in these early pieces, which also show at times his mature power, control, and confidence, even though the series is often marred by his groping, in apprenticeship, for style and literary attitude. For example, the inexperienced handling of the internal monologue of "Home," one of the earliest of the series, in no way would lead the reader to anticipate that only four years later William Faulkner would publish in *The Sound and the Fury* some of the best interior monologue ever written.

During the period when he was contributing these sketches to the *Picayune* Faulkner was hard at work on his first novel, *Soldiers' Pay*. According to friends he originally gave it the title *Mayday*, which he later used instead as the title of the unpublished allegorical work already mentioned. According to both Faulkner and Sherwood Anderson, Anderson brought the manuscript to Horace Liveright, who had just become Anderson's publisher. Liveright's house was then at the height of its success and was to bring out during the next twelve months not only Faulkner's first book and Hemingway's first, *In Our Time*, but also Anderson's *Dark Laughter*, Jeffers' *Roan Stallion*, Dreiser's *American Tragedy*, Roger Martin du Gard's *The Thibaults*, and editions of T. S. Eliot, Ezra Pound, O'Neill, and Freud.

But the firm did not reach its decision to publish *Soldiers' Pay* until late August, 1925, and by then Faulkner was no longer in New Orleans, having left

on his first trip to Europe. When he and Spratling
sailed from the Port of New Orleans on July 7, 1925,
as passengers aboard the freighter *West Ivis,* the
Picayune had already published twelve of his signed
sketches. He may have written and left with the editors one more sketch, "The Liar," and perhaps a second, "Episode." "The Liar" appeared in the issue for
July 26, while Faulkner was at sea, but he may have
written it aboard the *West Ivis* and mailed it to the
Picayune from Savannah, where the ship lay from
July 11 through July 14 to discharge cargo and take
aboard rosin and linters for the run to Naples. This
seems a good possibility, for though the *Picayune* had
published a sketch by Faulkner in every Sunday issue
during April and May, it had published none in June
or in July before the twenty-sixth, and former members of the staff doubt very much that the rather
hastily put together Sunday section of those days
would have held such a sketch in reserve. "The Liar"
is Faulkner's first published story with the rural setting he was to use so successfully in some of his greatest fiction. And one may speculate on the possibility
that once at sea he broke his series about the New
Orleans French Quarter to produce this story which
foreshadowed so much of his later work.

By the time "Episode" appeared in the *Picayune,*
August 16, 1925, Faulkner and Spratling had disem-
barked at Genoa, on August 2, and Faulkner was
beginnning to rove over much of northern Italy, visit-
ing Stresa; Piacenza; Pavia, where the quiet of the

city and the peace at the inn, Pesce d'Oro, delighted him; and the small village of Sommariva in the mountains near Lake Maggiore, where Faulkner lived during part of August with farmers, sharing their work and leisure and writing an unpublished travelogue.

In September, when "Country Mice" appeared in the *Picayune*, Faulkner, after travelling through Switzerland, had been living in Paris for some time, at 26 Rue Servandoni. As in New Orleans, he was only a few steps from the open space surrounding a church —Saint Sulpice—and from the freedom of a park, one more spacious than Jackson Square—the Luxembourg Gardens, where he spent much of his time.

For hours he helped children sail their boats on the pool, noting an old man with battered hat and enraptured expression who played with toy boats too— and who was to reappear years later in the final scene of *Sanctuary*, when children and a shabbily dressed old man are sailing boats in the Luxembourg Gardens as Temple Drake sits yawning there beside her father. But Faulkner, by no means suffering the boredom of Miss Drake, was writing. While the *Picayune* was printing the last of these sketches, "Yo Ho and Two Bottles of Rum," with its ocean voyage for which he may have drawn in small part on his trip to Genoa aboard the *West Ivis*, Faulkner was at work in the Luxembourg Gardens on a novel, and had just completed a short story. Years later a dowager was to ask him whether it was his practice to write by schedule or when the spirit moved him; he replied that it was only when the spirit moved him, but it moved him every day.

He returned from Europe to the United States at the end of 1925, reaching Mississippi in time for the Christmas holidays with his family. The next autumn he gave the following report of the winter, spring, and summer of 1926 to a reporter for the New Orleans *Item:*

William Faulkner, native of Oxford, Mississippi, who wrote "Soldiers' Pay" . . . returned to the Vieux Carre Sunday to plan a winter's work. Incidentally, he announced the publication of "Mosquitoes," another novel.

. . . Mr. Faulkner, sun-tanned from working as a fisherman on a Pascagoula schooner, and sucking an inscribed pipe, won last Spring when he shot a hole in one while acting as professional at the Oxford golf club, sat in an apartment in the old town and watched the rain-splashed roofs. . . .

He told of a summer spent working in a lumber mill, until a finger was injured, and then on the fishing boats of the Mississippi coast. At nights, after working hours, he wrote his new book.

Monday, he will return to Oxford for a short stay and at the end of September he will return to this city for the winter.

Faulkner was still writing poetry—as he had continued to do on his trip to Europe. A number of unpublished sonnets which survive from that period he dated at sea on the *West Ivis* and off Majorca and Minorca, and from Italy and Paris. Other sonnets, written in 1926, he dated from Pascagoula. For eight more years he occasionally published poems in periodicals; and *A Green Bough*, greatly revised from its original manuscript form, appeared in 1933. But in 1925 at New Orleans he had turned to fiction with full force. And in the three decades since, by developing many of the themes, techniques, thoughts, and feelings which appeared in these apprentice pieces, William Faulkner has published more than twenty volumes of fiction, much of it among the best in our century.

CARVEL COLLINS

Cambridge, Massachusetts
June, 1957

New Orleans

WEALTHY JEW

"I LOVE THREE THINGS: gold; marble and purple; splendor, solidity, color." The wave of Destiny, foaming out of the East where was cradled the infancy of the race of man, roaring over the face of the world. Let them roar: my race has ridden them. Upon the tides of history has my race * ever put forth, bravely mayhap foolhardily, as my ancient Phoenician ancestors breasted the uncharted fabulous seas with trading barques, seeking those things which I, too, love. Suns rise and set; ages of man rise and joy and battle and weep, and pass away. Let them: I, too, am but a lump of moist dirt before the face of God. But I am old, all the pain and passion and sorrows of the human race are in this breast: joys to fire, griefs to burn out the soul.

* In the original text this word is "may." Similar obvious typographical errors in the sketches from both *The Double Dealer* and the *Picayune* have been corrected without notation. When there has been any doubt, the original form has been retained and noted.

But from these bitter ashes which are I, heirs to my pleasures and pains will rise phoenix-like, for the blood is old, but strong. O ye mixed races, with your blood mingled and thinned and lost; with your dream grown tarnished and pointless, knowing not what ye desire! My people offered you a dream of peace that passeth understanding, and arid Syrian sands drank the blood of your young men; I flung you a golden coin, and you purchased martyrdom of Death in Ahenobárbus' gardens; ye took Destiny from the hands of my people, and your sons and my sons lay together in the mud at Passchendaele and sleep side by side beneath foreign soil. Foreign? What soil is foreign to me? Your Alexanders and Caesars and Napoleons rise in blood and gold, shrieking briefly of home, and then are gone as waves hiss curling on the beach, and die. No soil is foreign to my people, for have we not conquered all lands with the story of your Nativity? The seas of Destiny foam by. Let them! My people will crest them, mayhap to be swept like blown trumpets among the cold stars.

"I love three things: gold; marble and purple; splendor, solidity, color."

THE PRIEST

EVENING LIKE A NUN shod with silence, evening like a girl slipping along the wall to meet her lover. . . . The twilight is like the breath of contented kine, stirring among the lilacs and shaking spikes of bloom, ringing the soundless bells of hyacinths dreaming briefly of Lesbos, whispering among the pale and fronded palms.

Ah, God, ah, God. The moon is a silver sickle about to mow the rose of evening from the western sky; the moon is a little silver boat on green and shoreless seas. Ave, Maria, dream. . . . How like birds with golden wings the measured bell notes fly outward and upward, passing with clear and faint regret the ultimate slender rush of cross and spire; and how like the plummet lark the echo, singing, falls. Ave, Maria. . . . Ah God, ah God, that night should come so soon.

Orion through the starry meadows strays, the creaking Wain breaks darkly through the Milky Way's faint dewed grass. Sorrow, and love that passeth away. Ave, Maria! a little silver virgin, hurt and sad and pitiful, remembering Jesus' mouth upon her breast. Mortification, and the flesh like a babe crying among dark trees . . . "hold my hair fast, and kiss me through it—so: Ah, God, ah God, ah God, that day should be soon!"

Ava, Maria; deam gratiam . . . tower of ivory, rose of Lebanon . . .

FRANKIE AND JOHNNY

LISTEN, BABY, before I seen you it was like I was one of them ferry boats yonder crossing and crossing a dark river or something by myself; acrossing and acrossing and never getting nowheres and not knowing it and thinking I was all the time. You know—being full of lot of names of people and things with their own business, and thinking I was the berries all the time. And say, listen:

When I seen you coming down the street back yonder it was like them two ferry boats hadn't seen each other until then, and they would stop when they met instead of crossing each other, and they would turn and go off side by side together where they wasn't nobody except them. Listen, baby: before I seen you I was just a young tough like what old Ryan, the cop, says I was, not doing nothing and not worth nothing and not caring for nothing except old Johnny. But when that drunk bum stopped you and said what he said to you and I walked up and slammed him, I done it for you and not for me; and it was like a wind had blew a lot a trash and stuff out of the street.

And when I put my arm around you and you was holding to me and crying, I knowed you was meant for me even if I hadn't never seen you before, and that I wasn't no longer the young tough like what old Ryan, the cop, says I was; and when you kissed me it was like one morning a gang of us was beating our way back to town on a rattler and the bulls jumped us and turn us off and we walked in and I seen day breaking acrost the water when it was kind of blue and dark at the same time,

and the boats was still on the water and there was
black trees acrost, and the sky was kind of yellow
and gold and blue. And a wind come over the water,
making funny little sucking noises. It was like when
you are in a dark room or something, and all on
a sudden somebody turns up the light, and that's all.
When I seen your yellow hair and your gray eyes
it was like that. It was like a wind had blew clean
through me and there was birds singing somewheres.
And then I knowed it was all up with me.

Oh, Johnny!

Baby!

THE SAILOR

AH, TO HAVE PAVEMENT under my feet again,
instead of a motionless becalmed deck—motionless
as a rock thrust up from the sea's bottom, with
the very pitch starting from the seams and shrouds
and canvas heavy and dead in a breathless noon.
Or plunging and tacking off the bitter Horn! Icy
and stiffened the gear, and cold-blisters like boils
on every man's hands. But here is a stationary
world: she don't pitch and groan and boom, not
she! nor, scuppers under, race the howling gale.

Ah, lads, only fools go to sea—unless it be for
to change women occasionally. Surely a man cannot be satisfied with one kind for ever. There's your
wide-hipped Spaniard among the mandolins in the

smoky inn, your blonde Norse women, your pale
cold Anglo-Saxons. And I mind one I met beneath
the walls of Yemen; red haired, she was; and one
in the Chinee ocean: knifed three men. And where's
a man to make his final port, with all these from
which to choose?

A sound footing is good, and wine and women
and fighting; but soon the fighting's done and the
wine is drunk and women's mouths dont taste as
a man had thought, and then he'll sicken for the
surge and the sound of the sea, and the salt smell
of it again.

THE COBBLER

MY LIFE IS A HOUSE: The smell of leather is
the wall of my house. Three sides are dark, but
from the other side there comes faint light through
dingy unwashed windows. Beyond these windows
the world grows loud and passes away. I was once
a part of the world, I was once a part of the rushing river of mankind; but now I am old, I have
been swirled into a still backwater in a foreign
land, and the river has left me behind. That river
of which I was once a part. I do not remember very
well, for I am old: I have forgotten much.

Joy and sorrow—what mean these? Did I know
once? But joy and sorrow are the birds which whirl
screaming above the rushing flood: they do not

bother about backwaters. Peace I know in setting properly a nail, in fixing cunningly a sole, and in my wife. My wife? This bush of golden roses is my wife. See, how the ancient branches are twisted and gnarled with age, as this hand is twisted and gnarled and old. Yet each year it bears me sweet bloom, though it be as old in years as I.

Ah, Tuscany! and the belled flocks among the sunny hills long after the valley itself was in shadow! and feast days and dancing on the green, and she in her scarlet kerchief, her cloudy tossing hair and her sweet wild breasts arbored amid her hair! But we were promised, you see.

She and this rose and I were young together, she and I, who were promised, and a flung rose in the dust, under the evening star. But now that rose is old in a pot, and I am old and walled about with the smell of leather, and she. . . . and she . . . I have known joy and sorrows, but now I do not remember. I am old: I have forgotten much.

THE LONGSHOREMAN

"SHE WOULDN'T do what I asked her to, so I socked her in the jaw . . ." Jesus, look down: see dat barrel ro-o-o-ll! White folks says, and nigger does. Load dat steamboat, load her down; O steamboat, spread white wings and fly! Streaks of sunlight cutting the wall's shadow, slide up me, barring

my overalls my black hands with stripes of gold,
like a jail suit. Sinners in jail, sinners in heaven, behind dem bars of gold! I got wings, you got wings,
all God's chillen got wi-i-n-gs. . . . But, ah God,
the light on the river, and the sun; and the night,
the black night, in this heart. Oh, the black night,
and the thudding drums sultry among the stars. The
stars are cold, O God, and the great trees sailing
like ships up the rivers of darkness, brushing the
ancient stars forever aside, in vain. The earth alone
is warm, heated by the dead buried in it. But the
dead are cold, O lord, in the warm and the dark.
Sweet chariot, comin' fer t' cyah me home; sweet
chariot! wash me whiter'n sno-o-w!

Quittin' time, whistles boomin' and moanin'
like front row sinners at meetin' time. Ah God, the
singing blood, the sultry blood, singing to the fierce
fire in the veins of girls, singing the ancient embers
into flame! White man gives me clo'se and shoes, but
dat dont make no pavement love my feets. These
cities are not my cities, but this dark is my dark,
with all the old passions and fears and sorrows
that my people have breathed into it. Let this blood
sing: did I make this blood?

I got wings, you got wings; all God's chillen
got w-i-i-n-g-s-s!

THE COP

WHEN I WAS YOUNG, running about like a puppy or a colt, doing all the things which seemed to me grander than kings or even policemen could do (things which somebody always thought I oughtn't do) and being heartily wished dead by half the neighborhood in consequence, there was but one person in the world with whom I would have exchanged. Fellows there were who intended to be pirates, some would go west and kill Indians gallantly, blowing derisive whistle blasts at lesser adventurous mortals. But I, I would be a patrolman; in a blue coat and swinging a casual stick and with a silver shield on my breast, I would pace the streets away with the measured beat of my footsteps.

What to compare with this grandeur? To be the idol and fear of the lads, to be looked upon with respect by even grown people; to be the personification of bravery and the despair of criminals; to have a real pistol in my pocket! Later, in my adolescent years, this glamorous figure still paraded solemnly, filling my mind. I could see myself, huge and calm, negligently talking with admiring girls, being fed cake and pies and cups of coffee in snug kitchens, treading the lonely streets at night before dark houses where multitudes in slumber turn and sigh and safely dream, for I was there to guard them.

Or, foiling the murderer, shooting him dead in

the spitting darkness, and sorely wounded, being nursed to health again by a beautiful girl, whom I would marry.

But now that lad is grown up. Sometimes I think he still lurks somewhere within me, reproaching me because the man has been unable to give to the lad that high desire which life has promised him. But he sleeps easily; he does not trouble me often. . . . and what would you? life is not like that. Sometimes, pacing the dark and empty streets, he wakes and I am briefly troubled over the futile bargain a man makes when he exchanges a small body and a great heart for a large body and hardly any heart at all; but not for long. Certainly man does not ever get exactly what he wants in this world, and who can say that a wife and a home and a position in the world are not, after all, the end of every man's desire. Anyway, I prefer to believe that this creature fronting the world bravely in a blue coat and a silver shield is quite a fellow, after all.

THE BEGGAR

WHEN I WAS A BOY I believed passionately that life was more than just eating and sleeping, than restricting a man's life to one tiny speck of the earth's surface and marking his golden hours away to the stroke of a bell. What little of the world the ant can see is good to him; and I, with his vision

magnified an hundred times . . . . what would it
not be to the ant with my vision! Then multiply the
limit of my sight by the size of the earth . . . . and
there you are.

Ah, to have mounted heart and sight and sense
on such a sorry nag! The knight still would ride
forth, but his steed is old and not sure of foot any
more; other warriors on younger and lustier stal-
lions override and unhorse him, and now he must
whine and snarl with others whose steeds have failed,
over gnawed crusts without the relentless gates, in
the dusty road.

THE ARTIST

A DREAM AND A FIRE which I cannot control,
driving me without those comfortable smooth paths
of solidity and sleep which nature has decreed for
man. A fire which I inherited willy-nilly, and which
I must needs feed with talk and youth and the very
vessel which bears the fire: the serpent which con-
sumes its own kind, knowing that I can never give
to the world that which is crying in me to be
freed.

For where is that flesh, what hand holds that
blood to shape this dream within me in marble or
sound, on canvas or paper, and live? I, too, am but
a shapeless lump of moist earth risen from pain, to
laugh and strive and weep, knowing no peace until

the moisture has gone out of it, and it is once more of the original and eternal dust.

But to create! Which among ye who have not this fire, can know this joy, let it be ever so fleet?

MAGDALEN

GOD, THE LIGHT in my eyes, the sunlight flashing through the window, crashing in my poor head like last night's piano. Why didn't I close them damn shutters?

I can remember when I found days gold, but now the gold of day hurts my head. 'Tis night only is gold now, and that not often. Men aint what they used to be, or money aint, or something. Or maybe its I that aint like I was once. God knows, I try to treat 'em like thay'd want I should. I treat 'em white as any, and whiter than some . . . not calling no names. I'm an American girl with an American smile I am, and they know it.

There was wild blood in my veins; when I was young the blood sang like shrill horns through me. I saw women who had the bright things I wanted . . . . dresses and shoes and golden rings, lifting no finger to get them. And lights and sultry music, and all the bright chimaerae of the brain! And ah! my body like music, my body like flame crying for silken sheens a million worms had died to make, and that my body has died a hundred times to wear

48

them. Yes, a thousand worms made this silk, and died; I have died a thousand deaths to wear it; and sometime a thousand worms, feeding upon this body which has betrayed me, feeding, will live.

Was there love once? I have forgotten her. Was there grief once? Yes, long ago. Ah, long ago.

THE TOURIST

——NEW ORLEANS.

A courtesan, not old and yet no longer young, who shuns the sunlight that the illusion of her former glory be preserved. The mirrors in her house are dim and the frames are tarnished; all her house is dim and beautiful with age. She reclines gracefully upon a dull brocaded chaise-longue, there is the scent of incense about her, and her draperies are arranged in formal folds. She lives in an atmosphere of a bygone and more gracious age.

And those whom she receives are few in number, and they come to her through an eternal twilight. She does not talk much herself, yet she seems to dominate the conversation, which is low-toned but never dull, artificial but not brilliant. And those who are not of the elect must stand forever without her portals.

New Orleans . . . a courtesan whose hold is strong upon the mature, to whose charm the young must respond. And all who leave her, seeking the virgin's unbrown, ungold hair and her blanched and icy breast where no lover has died, return to her when she smiles across her languid fan. . . .

New Orleans.

February 8, 1925

Mirrors of Chartres Street

HIS VOICE had the hoarseness of vocal cords long dried with alcohol, and he was crippled. I first noticed him when he swung himself across my path with apelike agility and demanded a quarter for bread. His gray thatch and his eyes as wild and soft as a faun's, his neck muscles moving as smooth as an athlete's to the thrust of his crutch, stopped me; his garrulous assurance—"Say, you are a young man now, and you got both legs. But some day you may need a bite of bread and a cup of coffee, just a cup of coffee, to keep the damp out of your bones; and you may stop a gentleman like I'm stopping you, and he may be my son—I was a good one in my day, fellow." I had prided myself at the time on my appearance; that I did not look even like a prospective bum, wearing then tweeds which came from the Strand; but who knows what life may do to us? Anyway, to have such a breath fondly on one's neck in this nation and time was worth a quarter.

Fifteen minutes later I saw him again, handily swinging himself into a movie theater where was one of those million-dollar pictures of dukes and adultery and champagne and lots of girls in mosquito netting and lamp shades. Truly, his was an untrammelled spirit: his the same heaven-sent attribute for finding life good which enabled the Jews to give young Jesus of Nazareth with two stars in His eyes, sucking His mother's breast, and a fairy tale that has conquered the whole Western earth; which gave King Arthur to a dull world, and sent baron and knight and lads who had more than coronets to flap pennons in Syria, seeking a dream.

Later, from a railed balcony—Mendelssohn impervious in iron—I saw him for the last time. The moon had crawled up the sky like a fat spider and planes of light and shadow were despair for the Vorticist schools. (Even those who carved those strange flat-handed creatures on the Temple of Rameses must have dreamed New Orleans by moonlight.)

About the symbolical stolidity of a cop he darted and spun on his crutch like a water beetle about a rock. His voice rose and fell, his crutch-end, arcing in the street lamp, described a rectangle upon the pavement and within this rectangle he became motionless with one movement, like a bird alighting. "This is my room," he proclaimed hoarsely, "now, how can you arrest me, huh? Where's your warrant for entering my room, fellow?"

"I've sent for a warrant," the officer told him.

"But I'll get you anyway. You can't stay there all night; you got to leave soon to get a drink."

"I got a drink on me, fellow, and you know it."

"Yeh? Where is it?"

" 'S all right," replied the other, cunningly "you can't get it without a warrant."

The policeman leaned toward him, pawing at his sorry clothing.

"Take your hands off me," he screamed. He stood miraculously on his single leg and his crutch spun about his head like a propeller blade. "Arrest me in my own room! Arrest me! Where's laws and justice? Ain't I a member of greatest republic on earth? Ain't every laborer got his own home, and ain't this mine? Beat it, you damn Republican. Got a gov'ment job: thinks he can do whatever he wants," he informed the bystanders with hoarse cunning. He swept the crutch back to his armpit, and struck an attitude.

"Listen, men. I was born American citizen and I been a good citizen all my life. When America needs men, who's first to say 'America, take me'? I am, until railroad cut off my leg. And did I do anything to railroad for cutting off my leg? Did I go to railroad president and say, 'Say, do you know you cut off my leg?' No, sir. I said I been good American citizen all my life—all my life I worked hard. I been laboring man, and ain't every laboring man got his own room, and ain't this mine? Now, I ask you, one gentleman to 'nother, can damn Re-

publican come in laboring man's room and arrest
him?" He turned again to the cop. "You big coward, come on and arrest me. I got no gun; can't
shoot you if I wanted. Come in and arrest me!
Come on, now, I dare you. Can't no Republican
come in my room without a warrant."

Down the street, clanging among the shivering
golden wings of street lights, came the wagon at
last. As it stopped at the curb, he hopped nimbly
toward it. "Yes, sir," he croaked as he was helped
in, "I'm American citizen and laboring man, but
when a friend sends car for me, why, I'll go. Yes,
sir, never refused a friend in my life, even if he's
rich and I ain't nothing but self-respecting American citizen." Half-way in, he turned for recapitula-
tion. "I'm laboring man, own property in town, but
I got rich friends. Sam Gompers was my friend; he
wouldn't stood by and let damn Republican arrest
me, but now poor Sam's dead. Dead and gone, boys,
but he was my friend, friend all laboring men."

"Come on, come on," interrupted the officer.
"All right, Ed."

He was thrust abruptly in and the wagon
clanged away. "So long, cap," he shouted back, the
tires sucked over the wet pavement and around the
corner; clanging from sight and sound he went,
while his voice came hoarsely among the shadows
and intermittent light.

"So long, cap."

The policeman turned, his comfortably broad

back looked [*sic*] in the light, passed to dark and
from shadow to light again; then his heavy footfall
faded away.

And one thought of Caesar mounting his chariot among cast roses and the shouts of the rabble,
and driving along the Via Appia while beggars
crept out to see and centurions clashed their shields
in the light of golden pennons flapping across the
dawn.

February 15, 1925

Damon and Pythias Unlimited

THE CABILDO, a squat Don who wears his hat
in the king's presence, not for the sake of his own
integer vitae, but because some cannot, gloomed in
sinister derision of an ancient joke; within the portals Iowa wondered aloud first, why a building as
old and ugly could have any value; and second, if
it were valuable, why they let it become so shabby.
"I bet the city ain't painted it in twenty years. Why
don't they tear it down, anyway, and put up a modern building? They would have done that in Win-
terset years ago. These people in the South ain't got
the pep we have at all."

I pondered on the mutability of mankind—how
imaginative atrophy seems to follow, not the luxu-
ries and vices of an age as the Baptists teach us, but
rather the efficiencies and conveniences such as auto-
matic food and bathtubs per capita, which should
bring about the golden age. One almost believes
that the old farmer, who said he was not going to di-

61

lute his vigor by washing all over every day, was vouchsafed the true light.

A round, very dirty man somehow becomes involved here. I seem to have answered intelligently one or two of his remarks before becoming aware of him. His soft, melting brown eyes—like a spaniel's —bathed me in a moist, hot glow, his broad Semitic face shone, the very hat, once gray and worn rakishly upon his neck, seemed to have the same oily coating. Beyond his olive oil illusion, though, was something that puzzled me for a time. Then I got it: he smacked vaguely of—not horses, exactly, but of stables and racing swipes, and slumber in horse blankets.

"Stranger in town?" I told him yes, and his gaze became hotter upon me. "Noo Orluns nice place, huh?" I agreed to this also, and his gaze became mesmeric as he glibly mispronounced French names; he worked his way to and up Canal street, and then it came. No, I had not been to the races. His stare changed to a fond, protective amazement.

"Ain't seen the races? Why say, mister, to visut Noo Orluns and not see the races is like not eating a meal at Antony's (Antoine's?) cafe. Well, say, you're lucky, you are. I was just on my way out to the races now, and I'll be glad of your company. I know Noo Orluns like a book; I know the racing game as well as any fellow you'll meet. I'll be mighty glad to accommodate a stranger, but I'll be gladder still of your company. I been a chentleman all my life, see; and I know a chentleman when I see one.

Morowitz is my name," he ended, taking my arm
and removing my hand from my jacket, clasping
it heartily in his moist palm.

"Yes, sir, this is your lucky day, all right. I'm
sorry I ain't got my car with me. A good friend of
mine borrowed it off me this morning, but he'll meet
us at the track and I'll be glad to drive you around
and show you the city after the races. Come on, we'll
get a taxi. I wanta go to my hotel—you at the St.
Charles? No? Then we'll go on out."

I was interested in seeing if he really could get
in the St. Charles, even in a democracy, but I men-
tally promised that he should not shake my hand
again. A cab passed and he hailed it with arm and
voice. The driver slowed down, looked at the two of
us, and shouted back:

"Well, whatcher want?"

"None of that, now," my new acquaintance
shouted in turn. "Drive over here; my friend and
I wanta go to our hotel."

The driver weighed the two of us in his mind,
and then he addressed me.

"Are you with him?" I told him that I seemed
to be, and he drew up to the curb. My companion
leaped for the door, grasping the handle as the
driver reached to open the door from within, and
for a while the two of them mildly sported with it.

"Come on, come on, fellow. Whata you mean?
I'll report you for this."

"Well, turn the goddam handle loose, you ——
—— ——."

The door opened at last.

"Drive to the St. Charles, see? My friend and me are in a hurry."

"Well, get in, then. I can't take you or your friend nowheres until you get in the cab."

We sat back, but the driver still regarded us. "Well, where to? You wanta go riding, or to the police station?"

"To the St. Charles, I told you. That's where I always stay when I'm in town."

"Aw, come off, you don't live at the St. Charles."

"Listen, fellow; I'll have you arrested; I'll call a cop."

"You wouldn't no more dare call a cop than you'd dare go to the St. Charles." He looked at me. "Do you want to go to the St. Charles?"

We seemed to have been caught in some horrible vacuum of inactivity, to have no escape. "Do you really live at the St. Charles?" I asked him.

"Well, practically, see? My friend works in the Alhambra Baths right next door to the St. Charles, so what's the good of me staying at a hotel when my friend insists I stay with him, huh?"

The driver regarded him balefully. "Live at the Alhambra Baths, do you? Ain't been home in a week, though, have you?"

"Huh? Say, listen here, fellow—"

The driver addressed me again. "Take my advice, mister, and throw this bird out and go on where you are going, see?" I had about reached this conclusion myself, but I decided to carry on a bit longer. I asked him to drive us out to the race track, and we were off. Then I found how my companion's hat acquired that peculiar oily sheen. He removed it and mopped his face with it. He became voluble.

"Cheest, it's a shame what a chentleman must stand from these taxi drivers. I tell you, mister, I been a chentleman all my life and I ain't used to depending on taxicabs. But it happened I loaned my car to a friend today. Tomorrow, though, I'll call for you at your hotel. Listen, I'll put a car at your disposal all day, see? I'm a chentleman and I like a chentleman's company. Yes, sir, tomorrow they won't no friend of mine be insulted again by—" he nodded toward the driver's back and his lowered voice became obscene. I stopped him, revolted; and forbade his speaking again until we reached the track.

He hopped briskly out when the cab stopped, thrusting his fingers in his vest. "Got change for a twenty?" The corner of a bill showed in his fingers —a twenty.

The driver whipped out the meter receipt viciously. "Who you think I am—Carnegie?"

"I'll pay the cab," I interrupted. "You can get your bill changed at the gate."

"No, no," he said hastily, "I got some change— here you are, fellow. And when you drive chentlemen, learn to behave yourself."

The driver's reply was lost in the roar of his engine. "Get two," he continued to me, "I'll hand it back to you inside."

I got two tickets and we passed the turnstiles.

A race was just over, and through the pandemonium of the eight-to-ones we shoved our way, and out before the stands. The track flew smoothly past, swooped circling: a long rush and another turn and it swept into the home stretch—a graceful oval grassed with such a green as to seem poisonous; as if man or beast might take one bite and drop, stricken. The merry silks of riders flashed in the paddock and small puffy clouds fought a celestial handicap overhead.

"—said before, I know a chentleman when I see one, and I am proud of your acquaintance. Yes, sir; when I like a man I'm his friend, and I'll take care of him: he won't want for nothing. Now, this little jock I'm telling you about, he's my cousin, see? He's got inside information on every race run here. He's right, or he couldn't fool me—I been in this game too long to be took in. Listen, I followed the races all over the world: I been to 'em in Parrus, and in England I been to 'em; and I vouch for this little jock like he was my own brother, see? Listen, he couldn't fool you if I wasn't here taking care of you—you been around[,] I can see that. When you see him I bet you'll say he got the most intellichent face you ever seen: you watch what I say. But the boy's down on his luck right now. He's overweight a little and he's got a cough, not bad, but just enough so he can't take off this here overweight. So he ain't riding now.

"Now, he's got a jock friend in hospital: got no

money, no nothing. I swear I like to cried when he
told me about this poor boy laying up there with
doctors cutting on him all day long; got no money,
no nothing. I got a kind heart, mister, I admit it;
and when I like a man I like him, see? Now, what
you say we donate five dollars out of every bet we
win for this poor boy laying up in hospital? We
won't miss it, after the killing we'll make on these
tips of this cousin of mine. You and me, all we want
is a little sport: we don't need the money; but I
always say if you can have your sport and clean up
beside, why do it, I always say. Here he is now—
hey, jock!"

He approached, a thin lad in an extreme suit.
His face had a smooth, faintly girlish oval and his
eyes were kind and frank and gray, despite their
sophistication. But one look at his flat, spare shoulders and thin chest was enough to know that it was
no mere cough he had, poor boy. There was fore-
knowledge of certain death in his eyes. My companion, without a trace of humor, introduced his cousin,
Mr. McNamara. I took to him at once, and five dollars was quickly agreed on.

Four of his tips ran true to form in succession—
just tips. They both guaranteed the last one, though
—if the beast stood up he simply could not lose. I
here noticed that I was the only one risking any ac-
tual money. They were both quick to show me their
bets on paper.

"But you still have your twenty-dollar bill," I

reminded my first sponsor. "This race is a sure thing, you say. Why not plunge on it and recover?" No, no! This would not do. Even the angle of his hat became voluble. "Let me see your bill," I said. He demurred and tried to change the conversation.

"Let me see your bill," I repeated.

He produced it reluctantly, a twenty-dollar silver certificate issued by the Confederate States of America in 1862. I returned it to him.

Then the last race was run, and sure enough our horse won handily, netting me some two or three dollars after subtracting the promised fiver.

They both offered to deliver it, the boy with insistent politeness; while the other, still vocal, demanded, insisted, cajoled; pawing and rubbing my arms, trying to take the bill from my hand. We were beginning to attract attention.

"Listen, mister, I been a chentleman all my life. You think I would put anything over on another chentleman? Listen, you got me wrong. Listen, you give me that money and I'll—"

"Ah, beat it! Go on, you bum. Say, mister, don't listen to him. If he gets his hands on that money they won't nobody ever see a cent of it."

The other flung his hands heavenward. "Will you now listen to him! Insulting a chentleman and my friend before my very eyes! How much of that money now do you think he gives away yet? Listen: there ain't a worser one in Noo Orluns than him."

"Shut your mouth," the boy shouted, taking my arm. "Shut your mouth! He don't know you!"

"Don't know me! Who brought him here, huh? Did you? Say, listen, mister—"

"Don't pay him no attention, mister. I admit I ain't going to give this money to no one; I won't try to put nothing over you no longer. If you don't believe me, just keep this five and meet me tomorrow anywhere you say. I'll show you I'm square. Just keep the money and I'll meet you tomorrow and bring you out, and I'll treat you right."

The other screamed in utter anguish. "As God is my witness, he will rob you in spite of me. Listen, mister, say the word and I will call a cop to take up this noosance."

"Call a cop? You don't dare call a cop! Listen, mister—"

"Listen, mister! Don't you have nothing to do with that fellow. You don't know him, see? Listen: you give me your hotel number and I'll call for you in my car tomorrow, and we'll make a killing. It's four hundred ahead today I am, and tomorrow we'll clean up, see?"

"Four hundred ahead? Call for you in his car? Say, mister, did he say what kind of car he's got? Well, it was a Ford two years ago; I dunno what he calls it now. And he can't call for nobody in it because it's in hock for two dollars and a half. That's what he wants that five bucks for."

The other leaped upon him, shrieking. They struggled. Locked in close embrace they swayed about the floor. "You would rob me!" hissed the other, "you will give me nothing!" The lad flung him off. "Ah, I'll get your car out for you. But if you keep on I'll give you a smack in the jaw." The boy took my arm again.

"Listen, sir," he whispered hurriedly, "it ain't your money I want, it's your friendship, see? Meet me at the St. Charles at noon tomorrow with five hundred dollars, and we'll make a killing, sure. Don't fool with that bum no more. Keep the five, and I'll meet you at twelve sharp."

The other surged between us, breathing heavily. "Say, fellow, move off and let me speak to my friend in private, will you?"

The lad shook my hand, gave me a meaning look, and drew back. The other pawed me affectionately, trying to put his arms around my neck. I won, and he was forced to hiss his message from at least a foot's distance: "Listen, mister: I'm your friend, see? I've been a chentleman all my life; I'm accustomed to associating with chentlemen; me and you don't want to fool with no bums, see?" (Meantime the bum was flashing me knowing winks over my present confidant's round and oblivious head.) "You ain't gave him no money, have you? No? Well, listen: I'll call [for] you tomorrow, in my car, and we'll come out and clean up. What's your hotel?"

"Meet me at the St. Charles at twelve sharp," I told him. He released me and I moved away, leaving them glaring at each other across the empty room.

February 22, 1925

Home

A MAN sat on the curb. In his hands were a car-
penter's saw and a violin bow. The saw he held like
a violin and from the bow there rose a sound, a
resonant singing, half string and half pipe, which
the very atmosphere, which silence itself, seemed to
find strange and hard to digest: toying with it when
the bow ceased—a lilting provencal air played in a
virgin tonal scale, and somehow ambiguously martial.

* * *

Jean-Baptiste leaned motionless in a dark areaway, feeling the darkness flow past him down the
street, watching the quiet roof-tops cutting the sky,
watching the stars like cast roses arrested above an
open coffin. He was thinking of the dark corners
which men's destinies turn. His decision he could
still revoke, though, there was yet time; and this
very fact was a part of his unease. To get it over
with! To be either flesh or fowl, instead of being
neither, of having decided definitely to be the one

and then being forced to wait, and think. Thinking, indeed, lays lads underground.

If he could only forget that his decision might still be revoked! How simple things would then be. To decide, to act; and once and for all put himself beyond the pale. But as it was, he could see now how the heat of the moment, his present despairs, had tricked him. But it was not too late! There was still time.

True, there was his broken word. What would Pete and the General and Tony the Wop think of him? What would that thing within himself that knew not hunger nor sleep nor time, say to him? He had passed his word, you couldn't get around that. And he hated the nimbleness of his fingers, his knowledge of explosive, for he believed that had he been an ordinary immigrant living a dull life as an honest, unimaginative artisan, he would have escaped this temptation and the need of making this decision.

But it went further back than that. He thought of his boyhood in the South; of a thatched cottage near a forest where he roamed in the spring, of the airs of May within the chestnut trees. Remembering it in this kindhearted, impossible America was like remembering a song: through the twilight his waiting bowl of supper called him; there in the soft candle light he ate, and slept the night away on his pallet while the day of sun cooled [in?] his quick blood.

74

Of his wild and joyous adolescence he thought, and of his canny peasant mother, whose despair his young years had been, saying: "How this war is terrible! and how it has made a man of that Jean-Baptiste!"

A man, indeed! He thought of his platoon tramping newly through the mud of the Bethune road, a rose in its rifle barrel and a cigarette behind its ear. So new was he to war that he still expected something fine and grand: heart-quickening music and flags flapping out in the breeze; for two days he had carefully buttoned up the skirts of his coat, out of the mud. He even believed that the rain would cease tomorrow. But tomorrow he too believed that all fighting troops had been thrust into purgatory for some unnamed sin, there to wait until some vague Being could decide what to do with them—to send them to hell or not.

A policeman passed, paused to stare at him, then moved on. And Jean-Baptiste shivered, clasping his jacket more closely about his throat. How many more policemen would see him, and move on? How many hours, minutes, seconds, before, at the flash of a shield or a heavy footfall, he must dart skulking into hiding? How much longer would he be free, to walk the earth and drink the sun—be uncaged? Perhaps tomorrow he would clasp steel bars like a caged ape, panting for freedom.

This is not fear, he cried to his soul. Had I known fear I would not have stolen fruit from the vicomte's garden, when I was young; I could not have done what I did at Souchez.

But what does this signify? Have not my wits extricated me before?

Yes, says caution. But who can break the chain of circumstance and forge a link so cunningly that none can tell? Who breaks laws and goes unscathed? Mine is mine, and thine is thine; and woe to him who would act otherwise. Think, too, of Pete; of this Tony the Wop: how long have you known them? Ten days. Can you say what a man whom you have known only ten days will do under a given circumstance? Can you say what you yourself will do under a given condition?

But what have I gained by being honest? Work, hard work, in a country foreign to my nature. America, the Golden Land, they tell us. And what have I got? Food and sleep.

What do you want?

I want to gain a part of that beauty which shall not pass from the earth, of companionship, of love, perhaps—who knows?

Aye, who knows? Who knows what he wants, even when he gains it? But do you expect to gain it by robbing banks?

Why not? Money is everything.

Certainly, money is everything. But only money you yourself have earned. Can you take money not yours and buy contentment with it? Can you gain strength and sustenance from the food eaten by someone else?

Ah, but money is different. The food has been eaten, but the money has not been spent.

Good! You have now reduced it to its personal equation. Could you eat all the food you could obtain at this moment?

No.

Have you ever been without food?

Yes, for four days.

But you ate again?

Obviously.

Then, do you not see that He who gave you food when it was necessary will also care for your other wants? Who are you, to assume charge of a vessel, the destiny of which you cannot know?

But this begs the question. Yours is a comfortable belief to die with, but I am not interested in death: it is living I want; and life is more than food and sleep. So this does not settle it.

There came footsteps sounding in the dark and empty street, and Jean-Baptiste awoke from his problem. At last, he thought, his problem would solve itself, once Pete and the General came for him. But there was still time to withdraw! No! he told himself; I have passed my word: I will see it through. The danger was nothing, they had told him. He spoke little English and he was known as a quiet, law-abiding workman. But they could not understand that fear would not deter him, or that desire for gain would drive him into it. It was loneliness that had done it: the quick despair of his hot Southern temperament in an alien, heedless land.

But this was not Pete. A man passed carrying — of all things — a saw. He stopped at the corner and Jean-Baptiste cursed him: his mind was made up irrevocably. His five years of labor among strange customs had netted him nothing. Anything would be better than to continue in the way he was living, anything! Let it be luxury or let it be jail. He looked down the street again, waiting for Pete and the General and Tony; his hands felt as cunning and capable as separate organisms; the joy he had felt in handling high explosive in a shell factory after he was sorely wounded and incapacitated for action at the front, returned seven fold. The old sinister joy of compounding the volatile stuff, the benediction of a priest of the church who had blessed an entire day's output — "Let these shells scatter the enemies of France like chaff before the wind, O Lord!" — recurred to him. To take destiny like a bit of moist earth and mold a new man of it! Napoleon had done this — Napoleon, a round-headed, shrewd dreamer within whose veins ran the same fire, the same Southern sun, as in his.

Suddenly the empty street filled with sound, a resonant singing, half string and half pipe — a lilting provencal air somehow incongruously martial. Jean-Baptiste paused, stricken, and about him rose the land he called his; the wooded hills, and valleys, willow and tall chestnuts in the meadows where quiet cattle grazed or stood knee-deep in the water; of young love and nightingales among the chestnut trees after the sun had gone out of heaven and the intimate stars swam in a velvet sky. He saw the cottage where he was born, and ate and slept, sharp in the sun; he saw the wheeling candle light soft in a golden dusk beneath a single star like a yellow rose. He saw all this and knew that he had pursued a phantom into a far land; that destiny had taken him across seas so that he might see with a clear eye that thing which his heedless youth had obscured from him, which three years in the mud of Artois and Champagne could not make him see.

The strange yet familiar air rose and fell, and Jean-Baptiste lurched from his hiding place and went swiftly down the street. The musician sat on the curb, drawing his bow across his strange instrument; and so Jean-Baptiste passed swiftly on without disturbing him. At the end of the street the sky was rumorous with dawn, a new day.

March 1, 1925

Jealousy

"KNITTING AGAIN, eh?"

His wife raised her smooth, oval face and her soft eyes for a moment met his, then dropped to her work again. "As you see, caro mio."

"Knitting! Always knitting! Is it that there is nothing to be done here that you must knit at all times?"

She sighed, but made no reply.

"Well?" he repeated, "cannot you speak? Have you lost your tongue?" he finished roughly.

"But it was you, 'Tono mio," she replied without raising her head, "who insist that I sit here instead of in my little red room, as I desired."

"Bah! Someone is needed here; would you have me pay wages to one that you might sit all day like a great lady, knitting with your gossips?"

A waiter, a tall young Roman god in a soiled apron, came between them and placed upon the desk a ticket and a bill. The woman made the

change and gave the waiter a brief glance. He
looked into her husband's face—a level stare in
which his white satirical smile flashed, and withdrew. The other man's hand knotted into a fist
upon the desk and he stared at his whitening
knuckles as at something new and strange, cursing
in a whisper. His wife raised her head and regarded him coldly.

"Don't be a fool, Antonio."

He controlled his voice by an effort. "How
much longer will this continue?"

"Ah, that is what I would ask you: how much
longer are you to vent your ill humor upon me?"

"You, with your demure face," he whispered
fiercely, his hot little eyes blazing with bafflement
and sudden rage.

She looked quickly about them. "Hush," she
said, "people are looking. What do you want? Shall
I withdraw to my room?"

His face was dreadful. "No," he shouted at
last. He lowered his choking voice and continued:
"I will not have it, do you hear?" He lowered
his voice still more. "Listen. I will kill you, as
I love God."

She picked up her knitting once more. "Don't
be a fool," she repeated. "Return to your duties—
see, patrons arrive. You are insane."

"Insane or not, do not drive me too far."

"You are insane: you talk, you scream, you
curse—what?"

"You know well what."

"I? Have I ever given you cause or reason to go on so? Of what do you accuse me? Have I not been a good wife to you? Have I not at all times observed your wishes? You know well that I do not sit here night after night of my own wishes, of my own desires. This jealousy of yours is driving you mad."

"Bah! Be warned. That is all I say."

His gaze roamed from table to table as he sulked in his dirty apron, lurking among anaemic potted palms or serving his strange customers with servile insolence, and replying in snappish monosyllables to the greetings of old patrons. The tall, handsome waiter moved swiftly and deftly about, courteous and efficient. The husband compared the young man's supple grace with his own bulky figure and a fire gnawed in him. Once more the waiter approached the desk, his glance sweeping down the room rested briefly upon the husband's face, as he leaned intimately toward the wife.

The husband found himself walking in a red daze toward the two of them. He could not hear his own footfalls nor feel the floor beneath his feet. The waiter moved away as he approached, and his wife again sat bent above her knitting. Upon the desk was a china receptacle containing toothpicks; as he leaned upon the desk his fingers closed about the toothpick holder. The thing burst in his clenched hand amid a spurt of wooden splinters and a thin line of crimson was suddenly between his fingers and across the back of his hand.

"What did he say to you?" he asked; his voice to him seemed dry and light, like a broken egg shell.

The woman raised her head and her gaze met his full. Her eyes grew suddenly large, as though they would take up her whole face. "Listen," she said calmly, "you are insane. What would you have? Was it not you who put me here? I did not choose this." Her voice gathered warmth. "Am I to have no peace whatever? For six months now this has continued; day and night you have fretted and nagged at me; but now it must end. Either you come to your senses, or I leave you and return to my people. Take your choice: it is for you to make. But remember, this is the end. I have been a good wife to you, and I will still be if you but become again as you once were. But one more scene like this tonight, and I leave you."

He turned and walked away like a drunk man, or a somnambulist. He passed the waiter and the other's white, meaningless smile brought him to himself. He beckoned abruptly to the other and passed on through the kitchen and into a dark passage giving on an alley, where he waited, trembling. The waiter followed; in the constricted, shadowy place the other loomed above him, standing easily like a swordsman, looming above him though he was the bulkier man. Starlight was about them, and a faint wind stirred in the dingy alley.

"See," he said and his voice shook, "I know all; what is there between you?"

"Do you question me?" replied the other man.

"I will know: what is there between you?"

"There is nothing between us save the knowledge that you are crazy."

"Do not lie to me!"

" 'Lie?' This, to me? Do you give me the lie?" The younger man's body sprang like a poised sword, his fire seemed to make light the walls. The other quailed before him despite himself, cursing himself for his cowardice.

"But I must know! I will go mad!"

"You are already mad. Had you not been I should have killed you ere this. Listen, tub of entrails, there is nothing between us: for her sake whom you persecute, I swear it. I have said no word to her that you have not seen, nor she to me. If she be attracted to someone, it is not I. This I tell you because I am sorry for her, sorry for any woman who must be daily plagued by such as you."

"But what did you say to her but now, tonight?"

The young man slapped him, rocking his head upon his shoulders with two blows. The other staggered back. "I will kill you!" he screamed.

"You do not dare!" snapped the waiter, "you do not dare, save from behind. And what will the world say, if you do? Can you bear to have your wife call you coward? But I do not put this beyond you, hence I shall be on guard. And if you make the attempt, let it be successful, or God help you! Dog, and son of dogs!"

Alone again, the husband leaned against the cold alley wall panting, cursing in his rage and fear and hate. It was true: he did not dare. And he stared at the starred sky stretching like taut silk above the walled well of the alley, watching the same stars at which he had gazed in far-away Sicily, in his youth, when he had been a boy and life was clear and fine and simple; and that lads would stare wondering upon long after he and his dream and his problem were quiet underground.

He did not dare! The idea of assassination occurred to him, but he knew that he could not face himself afterward, his wife, that woman who had caused it all, whom he had taken but recently from her father's house and who was dearer to him than the world, than life itself, would never forgive him. He was almost middle-aged, and ugly and fat, while she, she was still young, and pretty. Was it any wonder that men were attracted to her as he had been? Was it any wonder that men should pause at her dusky oval face, her red mouth and raven hair, her black, black hair? And she— had she ever encouraged them? No! She had been a good wife to him, as she had said.

To go away, that was the answer—to take her to a new city; among new people they might yet live a second honeymoon. That was what he would do. He raised his face again to the heedless, flying

stars among which his problem had got so inter-
woven and tangled; allowing the cool night air to
play in his sweat-matted hair, and drew a long
breath. That was the solution.

His wife agreed almost at once. They discussed
the matter with her people and overcame their
objections. She had informed her parents from time
to time of his growing malady, so their decision
did not surprise them. He was industrious and, until
his present obsession took him, kind—a good husband in their eyes; too good to lose.

Once the decision made, he became his normal
self again. In fact, things went so smoothly that he
would have reconsidered, but his wife was firm.
So a purchaser for the restaurant was found in
the person of the tall young waiter. Relations between the two men were still strained and the older
man avoided the other. Whenever they were forced
to meet the younger acted as though nothing had
happened. His white, sinister smile was the same as
ever, yet the flash of his teeth in his dark face
had somehow the power to enrage the other, stirring
again in him old angers and fears he had thought
asleep. But the waiter was more pleasant and
courteous than ever; he insisted upon presenting
the signora with a parting gift, with such a polite
insistence that they could not refuse. And so at
last, one day at noon, the two men set out to choose
the gift.

A string of glass beads, or a medallion, the

young man wanted. And they entered a curio shop where such things were sold—an orderless jumble of pictures, vases, bric-a-brac, jewelry, firearms and brass. While the waiter examined and haggled over his prospective purchase the older man stood idly near by. The purchaser stood near a window, a string of beads looping from his raised hand, oblivious and defenseless. And it occurred to the other that, for the first time the two of them had been together in the same room, his enemy was completely at his mercy. And while his hand groped behind him among a litter of ancient weapons his caution rebuked him for the thought. This had all been settled; he was going away tomorrow, perhaps never to see the man again. But it would be so easy! was the reply. Just to pretend that this old pistol fitting snugly in my palm were a modern, a deadly machine—like this: and he slowly raised the rusted weapon while his thumb broke loose the hammer, and the spring which had slept for thirty years gathered itself. Like this! he whispered, aiming at the unconscious man he had once wanted to kill; and pulled the trigger.

The tiny room roared with sound and a lance of red flame leaped out like a sword. The young waiter crashed forward into a table of glassware, then to the floor; and the other man stood screaming with the burst pistol in his hand until a policeman plunged through the door.

April 5, 1925

Cheest

CHEEST!

When he taken me out to look over them dogs he had I says to him: "Say, whatcher doin' —startin' a glue factory?" I says. And he says, "Well, I dunno. I got a payroll full of lads like you now, but all of you together wouldn't make enough glue for one day's issue of thirteen-cent stamps. Bone fertilizer, mebbe, but not glue."

"Whatcher want," I comes back, "Jack Dempseys to ride them dray horses?"

"Naw," he says, "what I want is a few riders without no tongues. Then mebbe I can learn them something about this business."

"Listen, fellow," I says, "they can't nobody tell me nothing about the racing game."

"Nor about nothing else: I already seen that."

"Say," I says, looking him in the eye, "I'll quit you cold, see?"

"That's fair enough; that's how I found you—cold and broke, too."

"Say," I comes back, "you think you're smart, don't you?"

"I got to be," he says, "or I'd been in the poorhouse ten years ago, with a stable full of beagles and clever children all eating their damn heads off."

Well, anyway we talked on back and forth, him not making nothing offa me—I been around, see? I have ridden the best in the land and I ain't had enough mud in my face to roon my complexion, neither. Ask anyone who's followed the game, suggest my name to them—Potter's the name, Jack Potter. Yeh.

Well, I thought I might's well stick with him, a while, anyway. So we worked out them dogs. Cheest, they was a terrible lot. They wasn't only one of them stood out at all, but them others was so orful that you could have tooken a horse out of a ice wagon and he would have showed class in that bunch. So I ast the boss to let me and a swipe see what we could do with him.

Well, he said all right, that even we couldn't make him no worse than he was, and something about a little child shall beat them to the wire or something—kind of kidding, see? He knowed I was a rider right away, only he wouldn't let on. That was his way, making out like I was like the rest of them alley rats or that his plugs would go to sleep at the post or get out in front and fall down. I seen through all his talk about us jocks, though between I and you they was a sorry bunch.

Well, to make a long story short, I meet this jane, see? I was to a movie one night by myself, and next to me was this kid and her friend, both skirts. Well, they was showing a racing fillum. Cheest, it was terrible. They was one horse looked like a winner, with a decent jock he could of walked away. But this bird riding him done everything he could, setting too far back and letting hisself be dragged along by the reins, letting another skate take the rail on him and break his stride.

"Cheest," I says kind of out loud, "if a jock of mine ever done that, I'd shoot him."

Well, these two kids setting next to me giggled, and I seen the blonde one looking me over. "Cheest," I says, "it gives me a pain to see a good horse butchered like that farmer done that one."

She kind of giggled again. Cheest, she was peachy looking, and when she ast me was I a racing man, why I kind of livened up, talking pretty wide, see? They expect it. Well, we was going pretty well, then she says: "Gee, listen at me talking to a stranger. Excuse me, mister." And she clams up. I introduced myself, saying I wasn't one of them birds goes around trying to make janes all the time, and so she thawed out and introduced her friend and her friend introduced her, and then everything was jake.

Well, anyway I bought them a soda after the show, and made a date with them for a couple nights later, me to bring a friend. And so I fixed it up with the least crummy of them rats I was with, and we met them like they said and taken them out. This was the night before the race we was cocked for, trying this here skate we had been working out. So we told them jellies we couldn't be out late account of something fixed at the track tomorrow, and they said that neither could they be out all night. They was nice girls, see, but good sports. Well, we was to a place dancing and joking and so forth, having a good time; and while my skirt wasn't looking, I taken one of her—you know—garters, see, kind of for luck or something.

Well, she kind of raised a howl about it, but I says: "Aw, come on, baby, soft pedal it. You wanna get us throwed out?"

"But how'm I gonna keep it up?" she wails.

"Roll it, kid, roll it," I says. "I ain't a smoking man or I'd do it for you."

"Like hell you would," she says, when this big bird comes over wanting to know what it's all about, saying they runs a decent place and won't have none of that stuff.

"Say," I says, "who you think you're talking to?"

"I ain't talking to nothing," he says. "I know your kind. And one more yap outa you, and the street for yours."

"You think you're smart, don't you?" I says, but he didn't have no comeback for that. So she goes to the ladies' dressing room and fixes herself, and we beat it. Believe me, I give that guy a look, too, but he wouldn't take it up.

Well, to make a long story short, when I dressed for the race the next day, I put this here garter on my arm, just for fun, see? Them skirts was coming out to see me ride. Well, the boss seen the garter on my arm and he says: "Whatcher got there, engagement ring?"

"Ah, go to hell," I says, and he seen I meant it and shut up.

They was a big crowd out that day, milling around and hollering their heads off for the favorite. Our horse was kind of nervous to begin with, and the bands and hollering never helped him none. He didn't look so bad, though, compared with them other platers. I got a good position, and everything looked pretty good.

We got away in fine shape, and that gang in the stands let out a howl, and that dog of mine busted out of the pack like he'd been doped. I held him in a little until the favorite—the best-looking one in the race—come up, then I stayed with him. I never worried at all about the others.

We was neck and neck at the half; at the three-quarters the other horse drawed ahead a little. The stands was whooping fit to kill, and the other jock went to the bat. Well, I let my baby out and we come down the stretch riding the best I knowed to get everything they was in him, and to make a long story short, I raised my whip and brang that dog in a half-length ahead.

The ones that had played us for a long shot was wild as Indians. Some of them busted out on the track and got drove back for their pains, but most of them run to collect while the ones that didn't have us watched them.

I weighed out, and there was the boss, with his hat cocked over one ear, feeling pretty good, I'll say.

"Well, I guess you're satisfied with my riding now," I says.

"Yes," he says, "you done your best, and still come in ahead, didn't you?"

Well, say! What do you know about that? And more'n that, he's had that damn garter sewed onto my shirt. And he ast me to find that jane so he could contract with her to furnish garters for all his riders.

Cheest!

April 12, 1925

Out of Nazareth

BENEATH THE IMMACULATE SHAPES of lamps we passed, between ancient softly greenish gates, and here was Jackson park. Sparrows were upon Andrew Jackson's head as, childishly conceived, he bestrode his curly horse in terrific arrested motion. Beneath his remote stare people gaped and a voice was saying: "Greatest piece of statuary in the world: made entirely of bronze, weighing two and a half tons, and balanced on its hind feet." And, thinking of how our great men have suffered at the hands of the municipal governments which they strove to make possible, pondering on how green the trees were, and the grass, and the narcissi and hyacinths like poised dancers; blessing that genius who conceived a park without any forbidden signs, where tramps could lie in the sun and children and dogs could pleasure themselves in the grass without reprimand; I remarked to Spratling how no one since Cezanne had really dipped his brush in light. Spratling, whose hand has been shaped to a brush as mine has (alas!) not, here became discursive on the subject of transferring light to canvas; but not listening to him I looked at the faces of old men sitting patiently on iron benches as we slowly paced—men who had learned that living is not only not passionate or joyous, but is not even especially sorrowful. One, in a worn frock coat and a new pair of tennis shoes, explained to me the virtue of tennis shoes and borrowed pipe tobacco from me. And then, beneath sparrows delirious in a mimosa, and a vague Diana in tortuous escape from marble draperies in the background, we saw him.

Hatless, his young face brooded upon the spire of the Cathedral, or perhaps it was something in the sky he was watching. Beside him was a small pack; leaning against his leg was a staff. Spratling saw him first. "My God," he said, clutching me, "look at that face."

And one could imagine young David looking like that. One could imagine Jonathan getting that look from David, and, serving that highest function of which sorry man is capable, being the two of them beautiful in similar peace and simplicity —beautiful as gods, as no woman can ever be. And to think of speaking to him, of entering that dream, was like a desecration.

His gray gaze returned to earth and he replied easily to our greeting. "Hello," he said. His voice, his speech was Middle Western: one thought of wheat slumbrous beneath a blue sky and a haze of dust, along the land; of long, peaceful lands where the compulsions of labor and food and sleep filled men's lives. But he could have come from anywhere, and he probably had. He was eternal, of the earth itself.

"Going far?" he asked him.

"I dunno: just looking around."

He was hungry, but there was nothing of the beggar in him. He reminded one of a pregnant woman in his calm belief that nature, the earth which had spawned him, would care for him, that he was serving his appointed ends, had served his appointed end and now need only wait. For what? He had probably never thought of it. As all the simple children of earth know, he knew that even poverty would take care of its own.

He had worked (always with his hands) and liked it—liked to feel a worn hoe or rake handle in his palm, or a pick handle. "It's like holding a new shoe in your hands," he explained to us, "and when you are tired and your arms kind of ache, but you have a few dollars in your pocket." He liked to sleep in hay better than in a bed, he told us; especially when the cattle stand there after dark, making "night sounds" and you can smell milk, sort of, and the ground, too.

This developed over lunch at Victor's. He ate frankly, like an animal and though he employed his cutlery as one should not, there was nothing offensive about it—it was exactly what he should have done.

No, he told Spratling, he hadn't seen many pictures. But some he liked, when there were people like you see every day in them, or trees. Especially trees. Trees were nicer than flowers, he thought.

"So you are a writer?" he asked me shyly. "Do you write like this book?" From his sorry jacket he drew a battered "Shropshire Lad" and as he handed it to me he quoted the one beginning, "Into my heart an air that kills—" telling us he kind of thought it was the best he had seen.

"Why don't you go home?" I asked him.

"I will, some day. But that ain't why I liked that one. I like it because the man that wrote it felt that way, and didn't care who knew it."

"Is that so unusual?" I asked.

"Sir?"

"I mean, to feel something, and then write it exactly as you feel?"

Spratling here asked him if he had read Elizabeth Browning or Robert Frost. He had not—never heard of them. It seems that in Kentucky he had been given a meal in payment for which he had sawed wood; and, on leaving, a woman had asked him to throw away some old books and magazines. And among them he had found his "Shropshire Lad."

Again upon the street we had that feeling of

imminence, of departure and a sundering of the cords of contact.

"But you will need money," I remarked.

Spratling interposed. "Come to me tomorrow at three. I can use you for a model."

"But I may not be here tomorrow," he objected.

"Then take some money," Spratling suggested.

"Thank you, sir," he replied. "I'll get along all right. Thank you both, mister, for the dinner."

"Don't be a fool," Spratling rejoined.

"No, sir, I'll be all right."

Mankind is never as complex as we would like to believe ourselves to be. And so I said: "We will give you a dollar, and tomorrow you come to this address."

"But mister, I am not begging: I don't need your money. I will have a job by night."

"No, no; take the money, and call on us tomorrow."

"Why, I can get a job any time."

"Surely," Spratling replied, "but I want you to come to me tomorrow afternoon."

"But, mister, I may not be here."

"But won't you come, as a favor?"

His gaze brooded down Chartres street. "I guess I can. But I had rather give you something for the money." He turned to me. "Here, you are a writing man. I will give you this, and if I ain't there, you can have this for the dollar."

And this is what he gave me. There is bad

punctuation here, and misspelling: there is one word I have never deciphered. But to correct it would ruin it.

AN OPEN road stretching into the distance. Long lines of fences heming it in. Back of the fields, low hills in the distance. Not big hills but rolling formations overhung by a blue haze.

Cars whizz by. Cars filled with touring families. Cars with a single occupant. Delapidated Fords in which farmers drive to town. Cars filled with family parties bound to visit relatives in some nearby town.

With a pack on my back (consisting of necessary articles rolled in two blankets) I trudge along. The smell of farm house fires drifts down the wind to me. Pure air fills my lungs and gives an exhileration unlike any other that I know. The morning sun casts long shadows accross the fields. The dew of early morning glitters and the tall grass overhanging the side of the road is heavy with it. I am at peace with the world. Nothing matters.

I have eaten at a little restaurant. I have slept well on dried corn stalks between long rows of corn. I need not travel. I have no destination. I am at peace with the world.

I have my thoughts as a companion. Days spent alone have given me the habit of talking aloud to myself. Roosters crow, birds sing, a crow slowly wings his way from one distant wood clump to another. I seem to be in true communion with nature.

As the sun creeps higher the glare of summer is reflected from long rows of yellow corn. The road glistens and is a white streak which has no definite end at the horrizon. I sweat. Great drops roll down my face and settle in my open collar. The heat is good. It loosens the legs and warms the ground for the night's sleep.

Miles slide behind me. Now and again a car stops and I am given a ride. I do not ask for it. Why should I ask for rides when all around me is content? Those who wish to help me may do so, others may go on their way. I have no destination. Why should I hurry?

Noon comes and I lunch frugally on soup and milk. The hills that were before me this morning now surround me. The road no longer runs straight, but winds and dips among them. Trees overhang it and give a welcome shade from the noonday sun. Nature seems to plan my protection.

All afternoon I loll on the back seat of a speeding car (who's owner had invited me to ride). There is a dog in the back seat with me and we converse together as best we may. I scratch his ears and he cocks his head to one side and wags his tail. I stop for a minute to watch the changing form of some hill and he gently nudges me with his nose. My hand returns to his head and we resume our camradie.

The sun sinks lower and is hidden beyond the hill. There is still plenty of time to find a camp.

We come to a busy hill town and my heaviest meal is eaten. The food tastes as only food can taste to an appetite sharpened by a day spent in constant motion in the open air.

A slow tramp through the main street of the town and through the residential district brings me to the city camp. As I walk I look at the people restting on the porches, reading, talking and basking in the pleasant thought of a full day gone. Farther out I come to a region of stoops. Here shoeless laborers sit against buildings, one foot propped on a knee, smoking and talking shop, sports and politics. I catch words, sentences, fragments as I swing along.

Now and again a party sitting on a stoop stops its conversation to look at me. Perhaps a voice calls, "Where you from, kid?" and another, "Where you going?"

At the camp I find a place as far as possible from the rows of tents and spread my blankets. I wash my socks, which have become caked with sweat and the dust from the road. I brush my teeth and bathe as best I can.

I would ordinarily prefer to sleep in an open field or in a sheltering wood away from people. But tonight I desire the society of my own kind, so I stroll through the camp exchanging road gossip, stories, experiences, with motherly fat women washing dishes, wandering workers, business men out for a change, or a group of young men off for somewhere. Perhaps I help one of the women with her dishes and am rewarded with breakfast the next morning.

As it grows dark the fires stand out. The white walls of the tents reflect the light through, some music starts up and a party of young people start a dance on the porch of the small general store which serves the wants of the campers.

At the dance no introductions are necessary. We are all brothers and sisters. We are members of the fraternity of the open road, some for a short time, others forever.

Friendships develop quickly. Here is a German doctor [*sic*], a curious twisted little person with his hat on one side, playing some card game with a young Swede from the Dakotas who, it is evident, has lived in this country but a short time. The actor is going to the West to try the movies, the Swede is out to see the country. When he uses up his money he will sell his car and go to work.

A thin-faced, gangling Arkansan is discurrsing to several silent Westerners his difficulties in the Northwest. His youngest son, a boy of nine years, says to a playmate, "We pritt' nigh been all ova the country. We was in Vancouvar through California. We air headin' for the East now, and we'll get there prit' soon if Pop don't haf' to stop and get a job carpentering to buy us gas and food."

I HAVE given his story word for word, as he

wrote it. The spelling I have not changed, nor the punctuation. Some of the words mean nothing, as far as I know (and words are my meat and bread and drink), but to change them would be to destroy David himself. And so I have given it as it was given to me: blundering and childish and "arty," and yet with something back of it, some impulse which caused him to want to write it out on paper. And who knows? Give him time. He confided to Spratling and me, blushing, that he is seventeen.

But seeing him in his sorry clothes, with his clean young face and his beautiful faith that life, the world, the race, is somewhere good and sound and beautiful, is good to see.

He would not promise to call upon us. "You see, I wrote this, and I liked it. Of course it ain't as good as I wisht it was. But you are welcome to it." His young face stared into an ineffable sky, and the sun was like a benediction upon him.

"You see," he told us, "I can always write another one."

April 26, 1925

The Kingdom of God

THE CAR CAME swiftly down Decatur street and turning into the alleyway, stopped. Two men alighted, but the other remained in his seat. The face of the sitting man was vague and dull and loose-lipped, and his eyes were clear and blue as cornflowers, and utterly vacant of thought; he sat a shapeless, dirty lump, life without mind, an organism without intellect. Yet always in his slobbering, vacuous face were his two eyes of a heart-shaking blue, and gripped tightly in one fist was a narcissus.

The two who had got out of the car leaned within it and went swiftly to work. Soon they straightened up, and a burlap bundle rested on the door of the car. A door in the wall near at hand opened, a face appeared briefly and withdrew.

"Come on, let's get this stuff out of here," said one of the men. "I ain't scared, but there ain't no luck in making a delivery with a loony along."

"Right you are," replied the other. "Let's get done here: we got two more trips to make."

"You ain't going to take him along, are you?" asked the first speaker, motioning with his head toward the one lumped oblivious in the car.

"Sure. He won't hurt nothing. He's a kind of luck piece, anyway."

"Not for me he ain't. I been in this business a long time and I ain't been caught yet, but it ain't because I been taking no squirrel chasers for luck pieces."

"I know how you feel about him—you said so often enough. But like it was, what could I do? He never had no flower, he lost it somewheres last night, so I couldn't leave him to Jake's, going on like he was for another one; and after I got him one today I couldn't of put him out nowheres. He'd of stayed all right, till I come for him, but some bull might of got him."

"And a —— good thing," swore the other. "Dam'f I see why you lug him around when they's good homes for his kind everywheres."

"Listen. He's my brother, see? And it's my business what I do with him. And I don't need no —— that wears hair to tell me, neither."

"Ah, come on, come on. I wasn't trying to take him away from you. I'm just superstitious about fooling with 'em, that's all."

"Well, don't say nothing about it, then. If you don't wanta work with me, say so."

"All right, all right, keep your shirt on." He looked at the blind doorway. "Cheest, what's the matter with them birds today? Hell, we can't wait here like this: be better to drive on. Whatcher say?" As he spoke the door opened again and a voice said: "All right, boys."

The other gripped his arm, cursing. At the corner two blocks away a policeman appeared, stood a moment, then sauntered down the street toward them. "—— here comes a bull. Make it snappy now; get one of them fellows inside to help you and I'll head him off and keep him till you get unloaded." The speaker hurried off and the other, glancing hurriedly about, grasped the sack resting upon the door of the car and carried it swiftly through the doorway. He returned and leaned over the side of the car, trying to lift up the other sack onto the door. The policeman and his companion had met and were talking.

Sweat broke out on his face as he struggled with the awkward bundle, trying to disengage it from the floor of the car. It moved, but hung again despite his utmost efforts, while the body of the car thrust against his lower chest, threatened to stop his breathing. He cast another glance toward the officer. "What luck, what rotten luck!" he panted, grasping the sack again. He released one hand and grasped the idiot's shoulder. "Here, bub," he whispered, "turn around here and lend a hand, quick!" The other whimpered at his touch, and the man hauled him half about so that his vacant, pendulous face hung over the back seat. "Come on, come on, for God's sake," he repeated in a frenzy, "catch hold here and lift up, see?"

The heavenly blue eyes gazed at him without intent, drops of moisture from the drooling mouth fell upon the back of his hand. The idiot only raised his narcissus closer to his face. "Listen!" the man was near screaming, "do you wanta go to jail? Catch hold here, for God's sake!" But the idiot only stared at him in solemn detachment, and the man raised up and struck him terribly in the face. The narcissus, caught between fist and cheek, broke and hung limply over the creature's fist. He screamed, a hoarse, inarticulate bellow which his brother, standing beside the officer, heard and came leaping toward him.

The other man's rage left him and he stood in vacant and frozen despair, when vengeance struck him. The brother leaped, shrieking and cursing, upon him and they both went to the pavement. The idiot howled unceasingly, filling the street with dreadful sound.

"Hit my brother, would you, you ——," panted the man. The other, after the surprise of the assault, fought back until the policeman leaped upon them, clubbing and cursing impartially. "What in hell is this?" he demanded when they were erect and dishevelled, glaring and breathless.

"He hit my brother, the ——."

"Somebody certainly done something to him," snapped the officer. "For Pete's sake, make him stop that racket," he roared above the deafening sound. Another policeman thrust through the gathering crowd. "What you got here? Mad cow?" The idiot's voice rose and fell on waves of unbelievable sound and the second policeman, stepping to the car, shook him.

"Here, here," he began, when the brother, breaking from the grasp of his captor, leaped upon his back. They crashed against the car, and the first officer, releasing the other captive, sprang to his aid. The other man stood in amazement, bereft of power to flee, while the two officers swayed and wrestled with the brother, stretching the man, screaming and kicking, between them until he wore himself out. The second policeman had two long scratches on his cheek. "Phew!" he puffed, mopping his jaw with his handkerchief, "what a wildcat! Has the whole zoo broke out today? What's the trouble?" he roared above the magnificent sorrow of the idiot.

"I dunno exactly," his partner shouted back. "I hear that one in the car bellow out, and look around and here's these two clawing in the gutter. This one says the other one hit his brother. How about it?" he ended, shaking his captive.

The man raised his head. "Hit my brother, he did. I'll kill him for this!" he shouted in a recurrence of rage, trying to cast himself on the other prisoner, who crouched behind the other policeman. The officer struggled with him. "Come on, come on; want me to beat some sense into you? Come on, make that fellow in the car stop the howling."

The man looked at his brother for the first time. "His flower is broken, see?" he explained, "that's what he's crying about."

" 'Flower?' " repeated the law. "Say, what is this, anyway? Is your brother sick, or dead, that he's got to have a flower?"

"He ain't dead," interjected the other policeman, "and he don't sound sick to me. What is this, a show? What's going on here?" He peered into the car again and found the burlap sack. "Aha," he said. He turned swiftly. "Where's the other one? Get him quick! They've got liquor in here." He sprang toward the second man, who had not moved. "Station house for yours, boys." His companion was again struggling with the brother, and he quickly handcuffed his captive to the car, and sprang to the other's aid.

"I ain't trying to get away," the brother was shrieking. "I just want to fix his flower for him. Lemmego, I tell you!"

"Will he quit that bellowing if you fix his flower?"

"Yeh, sure; that's what he's crying for."

"Then for God's sake fix it for him."

The idiot still clutched his broken narcissus,

weeping bitterly; and while the officer held his wrist the brother hunted about and found a small sliver of wood. String was volunteered by a spectator, who fetched it from a nearby shop; and under the interested eyes of the two policemen and the gathering crowd, the flower stalk was splinted. Again the poor damaged thing held its head erect, and the loud sorrow went at once from the idiot's soul. His eyes were like two scraps of April sky after a rain, and his drooling face was moonlike in ecstasy.

"Beat it, now," and the officers broke up the crowd of bystanders. "Show's all over for the day. Move on, now."

By ones and twos the crowd drifted away. And with an officer on each fender the car drew away from the curb and on down the street, and so from sight, the ineffable blue eyes of the idiot dreaming above his narcissus clenched tightly in his dirty hand.

The Rosary

MR. HARRIS HATED two things: his neighbor, Juan Venturia, and a song called "The Rosary." He took a fierce delight in never having been able to decide which he hated most. On those days when Venturia, cleaning his premises, dumped trash and tin cans—and once a dead cat—into Mr. Harris' areaway; or when one of Mr. Harris' prized chickens got onto Venturia's premises and suffered abrupt and complete extinction in consequence, he knew that he hated Venturia with a passion unknown to this world. But, when forced by his wife or daughters to attend one of those musical functions where foreigners with uncurried manes who could neither speak nor play in English, scraped dolefully away at fiddles, he knew that nothing anywhere could be worse than "The Rosary"—or any other tune, as far as he was concerned.

Juan Venturia, on his part, neither knew nor cared a whoop in hades about "The Rosary." He was unmarried, hence he didn't have to attend concerts, which served to make Mr. Harris more furious than ever. He thought the police should do something about it. Venturia found life good: there was money to be made, he met his friends nightly at a certain restaurant, he went and came as he liked. So he could save all his hatred for Mr. Harris and Mr. Harris' chickens, and his cat and his house, and everything that Mr. Harris owned or liked.

Life was indeed good. He could watch for Mr. Harris and whistle "The Rosary" while the other passed, he answered advertisements in magazines, having samples of mange and tobacco cures, toilet articles, cooking utensils, etc., sent to Mr. Harris C.O.D., and then sat in his chair and heard Mr. Harris rave terribly and in vain.

One day Mr. Harris did not appear at his usual hour; and Venturia, being unable to whistle "The Rosary" as he passed, felt that his enemy had deliberately injured him. But when he heard later that Mr. Harris was ill, he was suffused with glee. For a whole day he sat chuckling in his shop, breaking occasionally into shouts of laughter, to the consternation of his patrons. At the cafe that evening he was gay and merry, keeping his companions in roars of laughter.

Later, as he lay in bed, heaving and chuckling, a terrible thought struck him. Suppose his enemy were to die! Be beyond the reach of his hatred! He thought of all the chances of really doing something mean to Mr. Harris, and his joy left him. Just killing a few dirty yellow chickens and throwing a little garbage into his areaway—what were these, compared to what he might have done? Nothing, and less than nothing. These tricks were childish, a ten-year-old boy could have thought of these. But he, Venturia, was a man: he should have thought of something to have driven his foe to bed and made him long to die. And now, it was too late. His enemy was beyond his reach, there was nothing he could do to injure him. He cursed himself, racking his brains.

To let his enemy escape like this! If Mr. Harris died he, Venturia, would be miserable: he would be forced to die also and follow the other to purgatory and so finish the business which he had criminally neglected in life. If there were but something, anything, he could do before his foe foiled him forever by dying! He tossed and turned, sleeping fitfully and waking again to groan and mourn his lost opportunities. How many things he could think of now, when it was too late! He could still set fire to Mr. Harris' house, but this meant the risk of imprisonment. Hence part of his despairing rage was transferred to the police. Chance, government, everything was against him. . . .

He waked suddenly from a fragmentary dream. Dawn was grayly at the window. A wagon rattled past and a ship bellowed hoarsely from the river. Venturia sprang from his bed, stifling a cry of victory. He had it at last: he had dreamed it. So simple it was, and so grand! It would make his enemy pant for death; it was colossal. There was only one flaw in it. "Why, oh why, did I not think of this before?" he moaned. "I could have driven him crazy, I could have made him as an idiot, mewling and weeping, beating his head upon the floor!"

He would have run from his house to accomplish it immediately, then his calm sense returned. So he crawled back in his bed and lay nursing his scheme in fiendish, impatient glee, until morning came. He made a hurried breakfast, locked his shop, and hastened up Royal street, like one possessed. Before a pawnshop he paused, then disappeared within it. A few minutes later he reappeared carrying a longish, bulky object wrapped in newspaper under his arm. He turned off Royal street in the opposite direction from his shop, and all that day his shop remained locked and closed, and for a week his old haunts knew him not.

Mr. Harris lay at home in the throes of pneumonia. In the intervals of consciousness he found time to wonder what Venturia was doing, what he was up to. He knew the other would not let him alone to die in peace. He expected anything, something violent in the way of noise, whatever his enemy's childlike mind could conceive. But day after day passed, and nothing happened, and Mr. Harris became a trifle fretful over it. It was like waiting for an explosion which for some reason is delayed, expecting it each moment and flinching, until even the explosion becomes preferable.

"Wish he'd get it over with," thought the sick man fretfully. "But it won't be long," he reassured himself. "I'm about gone, and the beast can't get at me much longer, thank heaven. And thank heaven, I won't have to attend any more concerts. Death ain't so bad, after all," mused Mr. Harris, like many a man before him.

And what of Venturia? Those companions whom he was wont to meet and who saw him no longer, asked this question among themselves. But no one had seen him. His shop saw but little of him, and when he was in he sat staring raptly at the wall, his hands held stiffly before him one above the other at the height of his belt, while his dirty fingers waggled stiffly as though in some clumsy, yet intricate sign language. And passersby stared in amazement and the little blackguard boys with pleasure, at his intent, corrugated face and the rigid genuflections of his hands. At twilight he closed his shop, and carrying his lumpy bundle, he left, returning about midnight to sleep and chuckle and dream of his revenge.

At last came the day. Now that the hour was come all Venturia's excitement was gone. He was calm, awaiting his destiny. He rose, breakfasted leisurely, shaved and donned his Sunday suit and a white shirt. He shined his shoes and plastered his hair to his head with scented oil. Then picking up his bundle he repaired to his areaway directly beneath the window where he knew the sick man lay.

He raised his eyes and gloated upon the dumb wall of his enemy's house. It seemed to him that his gaze could pierce the walls, that he was in the very room where the other lay. Then, slowly, he unwrapped the soiled and tattered newspaper from his engine of vengeance.

Mr. Harris, though, was no longer in that room. His wife was there, and his daughters were there, beside the bed where Mr. Harris had lain and waited for whatever Venturia might decide to perpetrate next; but Mr. Harris himself had gone where the Venturias of the world could not bother him more, where slain chickens and even dead cats in his areaway were of no importance.

From beneath the window there rose suddenly the excruciating, succulent bray of a saxophone blown by a rank amateur. The tune seemed to be nothing, the tune seemed to be two tunes played at the same time: it blatted and mewed and wept, filling the morning and spilling the dusty sparrows tumultuously from the eaves.

Only Venturia and Mr. Harris could have known that it was "The Rosary."

May 10, 1925

The Cobbler

YOU WAN' GETTA thees shoe today? Si, si. Yes, I coma from—tella in my tongue? Buono signor.

Yes, I come from Tuscany, from the mountains, where the plain is gold and brown in the barren sun, and the ancient hills brood bluely above the green and dreaming valleys. How long? Ah, who knows? I am very old: I have forgotten much.

When I was young I lived much in the sun, tending goats. The people of my village labored among the vineyards sprawled upon the slopes drinking up the sun; as I followed my flocks I could see them, the bright colors, and hear the faint, sweet singing like the broken flight of golden birds. I munched my bread and cheese at noon, and drowsed among the sun-swelled rocks until the air and heat and silence sent me to swim in warm slumber. And always at sunset an ancient father of goats roused me with his cold nose.

And she was young also. Almost daily we met

131

among the hills, I with my goats and she having slipped away from her set tasks, to idle in the sweet sun. How like a little goat she was, leaping chasms at which I paused, taking what pleasure the day offered, knowing that punishment awaited her for slipping away, knowing that she could slip away again on the morrow. And so it was.

And ah, how she bloomed; how, when we both become [sic] older, how the eyes of the young men did follow her. But I had not been idle: I had labored, I had goats of my own; and so we were promised: it was all arranged. She no longer climbed the morning hill with me now. She must remain at home, baking and making cheeses of goats' milk, treading out the grapes in the autumn, staining her sweet white feet with the sunned purple juice, as though the dear Christ Himself had bathed her feet in His own dear blood, as I would gladly have done.

And on the feast days, in her scarlet kerchief, how she shone among the others! Her tossing hair in the dance, her sweet wild breasts arbored amid her hair! It is no wonder, signor, that the young men panted and wept for her, for where in our valley, in all the world, was her equal? But we were promised: it was all arranged.

After the fiddles were silent and the sun had dropped beyond the dreaming purple hills and the bells chimed across the dusk like the last golden ray of the sun broken and fallen echoed among the rocks, we often walked. The belled flocks were stilled

and candles guttered gold about the supper tables,
and we walked hand in hand while the stars came
out so big, so near—it is not like that in your
America, signor.

She often chided me on my backwardness in
the dance or with the girls—how I labored and
saved, and at the dancing looked but diffidently on
while others danced and wooed her in their colored
shirts and copper flashing rings. And she often
teased me, saying that one of her beauty deserved
better than I. With which I agreed, for where in
our valley was her equal? But we were promised.

Am I married? No, signor. The saints had
willed otherwise. She? . . . . (I am old: I forget
easily.) Ah. There was one came to our village:
a grand signor in velvet and with rings of pure
gold—like a lord he was, with his dark, proud
look, like a thin sword in a velvet sheath. He, too,
saw her upon the green, saw her like a sweet
music one has forgot, and he, too, became as the
other young men. And she, when she saw that
grand one with eyes for none save her, she danced
as none of that village had ever danced. They who
watched were hushed as though they had looked
briefly into heaven, for she was like the music
of a hundred fiddles become one white and scarlet
flame, she was like to make the sleeping saints
in heaven wake sad, and know not why. But what
would you? He wore velvet, and his rings were
of pure gold. But then, we were promised.

That night, amid the hills where I walked, the great stars were loud as bells in the black sky, loud as great golden-belled sheep cropping the hill of heaven, like the great old ones among goats who had seen much sorrow, and still browsed on. But soon the night was gone away, and the stars were gone, and the hills were azure and gold in the morning. And there, in the dust beneath her window, where I was wont to pause briefly of a morning, was this yellow rose. It was not then as it is now: now it is old and black and twisted, as I am; but then it was green and fresh and young. Yes, I have kept it. When she returns she will doubtless desire me to have kept it; had I not kept it, she will be sad. And it has well repaid me: yearly it renews itself—like this. The saints are very good.

What? Was I sad? I do not know. I have known joy and sorrow, but now I do not remember. I am very old: I have forgotten much.

You getta thees shoe today. Si, si.

May 17, 1925

Chance

HIS ROUND, FATUOUS FACE was smug with self-esteem. He had completely forgotten that he had not wherewith to buy his next meal: why should he? The Lord will provide. And now with his cuffs turned and his collar on wrong side out, his shabby suit shaken into something resembling its former shape, why should he? He looked as good as any of them.

"Mebbe they'll think I'm a racing man, with a roll on my hip would choke a ox," he said to himself, sneaking looks at his passing image in the shop windows. Nowhere on Royal street could he see another flat that looked as good as he did. He took another long look at himself in a window, and collided with another body.

"Listen, brother," this one began, "I ain't ate since three days ago. Can't you gimme the price of a cup of coffee? Listen, I been drunk: I admit it; but now I'm trying to sober up, see? How about

137

a cup of beefstew to sober up on? God will see it
from heaven, and He'll reward you, guy."

"Hell," he replied, "you can't buy a drink here
for two bits, can you?"

His new friend became expansive. "Why, sure,
if you've got the price. Listen, I can take you to a
nice quiet family place, where I'm well known, see?
Anybody I bring there is all right. Of course you've
got to have the price."

He took the other's arm; and the beggar
drooped upon him affectionately. "Let's go," he
said.

They had a drink.

There were two other guests present, a truck
driver and a very ex something that smacked
vaguely of the sea, who joined him. "Let her ride,"
he said, with that grandeur only to be achieved by
one with brass and no money.

They had another—three of them did. The
beggar was ignored this time, and he immediately
became vocal.

"Come on, men," he said, "lemme in on this.
I'll buy a round—see if I don't."

"We can't wait that long," murmured the
truck driver, and the beggar became insistent.

"Listen," he said, grasping his patron's arm,
"listen. Who brought you here? Who showed you
the most convenient place in New Orleans? I did.
And yet you let your rich friends treat me like
I was a dog or something. Listen, I'm a self-respect-

ing seaman waiting for a berth. Sure, I ain't
got any money, but I wouldn't treat a dog like
you're treating me. Jest one drink, men, before I
go down to the shipping office." He pawed his
benefactor with passion.

"Get to hell away from me," said that hero,
flinging him off violently. The beggar fell, and got
slowly to his feet; and as the other turned again
to the bar, leaped upon his back. They went down
together; he rose and tried sincerely to kick the
beggar's head off, but the two of them were grasped
and ejected bodily into the street. They sat up,
under the disgusted stare of a policeman.

He stated his case to a bored desk sergeant;
the beggar stated his case, aloud and still louder.

"My God," broke in the sergeant, "get 'em out
of here. I can't stand this any longer."

"Where to, sergeant?" asked the patrolman.
His sister had not got married the night before.

"Anywhere!" roared the official, "just so they
can't talk to me any longer."

So once more he found himself in the gutter.
He sat for a while stupidly staring at the blank
door of the station. His hand rested on something
round and hard: he closed his fingers on it and
raised it from the mud. In his hand was a penny—
a copper cent.

A copper cent. What in the world could you
buy with a copper cent? Why, chewing gum, pro-
vided he could find one of those gum vending ma-

chines; or he could get weighed for a cent; or he could buy a box of matches for it. So he picked himself up, wiping the mud from his clothes. Alas! he no longer looked as if he might have a roll on him.

As he approached Canal street, looking for a gum vending machine, a running man plunged by him, followed by an excited chase crying "Stop thief!"

He joined the pursuit, and the fleeing man sped past a corner. A cop stepped out; they collided and the quarry went down. The policeman grasped his collar before he could rise. The pursuit panted up.

"What's going on here?" asked the law.

A breathless pursuer explained.

"This feller stole a five-dollar goldpiece from a newspaper seller. He took a paper, put down a nickel, and picked up a penny and a five-dollar goldpiece the boy had on his shelf."

The policeman shook his captive. "How about it, huh?"

"Honest, officer," the man pleaded, "I never meant to take his money. I picked it up by mistake, and just as I was about to tell him about it, he falls backward into the gutter and starts hollering 'Stop thief!' And I ran before I thought."

"Have you still got it?"

"Sure: here it is. I was going to give it back to

him. Honest, I ain't no thief: I got a job here in town—lived here all my life."

The officer looked at the gathering crowd. "Where's the newsboy?" he asked, and his eye fell on our hero. "You, there, with the mud on you: is this your goldpiece?"

He felt himself thrust forward, and the original informant averred: "Sure, officer, this is the one."

The policeman examined our hero narrowly. "I'm a good mind to take you both up, but this bird"—shaking his captive—"says it was a mistake. Whatcher wanna do? Have him arrested, or take your money back and let him go?"

"I'll take the five," he replied, and the crowd murmured approbation.

The culprit passed over the goldpiece.

"Here, here," the policeman interjected, "you owe him a penny yet."

From his muddied clothes he took the penny he had found and gave it to the other. The crowd melted away, as such crowds do, and he was left staring at the five-dollar goldpiece in his hand.

Five dollars. What to do with five dollars? He thought immediately of five dollars' worth of food. But it would be foolish to spend gold money for food when there were so many other ways of getting food. This seemed to be his lucky day, anyhow. His lucky day . . . . his lucky day. . . .

When your luck is good, why, force it. Any

141

fool knows that. And there, on a billboard on Canal street, was a list of today's entries. And in the third race was a horse named Penny Wise. It was a portent: an indication from the very gods that run the world. So he put his five on Penny Wise at forty to one. And Penny Wise broke out of the whole field like a scared rabbit.

Two thousand dollars. What couldn't you buy with two thousand dollars? He sat in a park, trying to recall all the things he had once wanted. Funny how when you're broke you can think of any number of things you'd like to buy, but as soon as you have the price you can't recall to save your life what it was. "So I guess I'll buy a car," he said. "Mebbe that's what I want."

"Listen," a friend said to him, "lemme take that money for you. You'll run through it in a month, and then you'll be on the street again. Lemme take care of it for you."

"Sure," he said; and had his clothes cleaned and pressed for eighty-five cents; and he bought a lemon-colored sports car for one thousand nine hundred and eighty-nine dollars. A kind salesman undertook to teach him to drive it. He caught on quite fast—so fast that he drove out Jackson avenue and off the Jackson avenue dock into the river at about forty miles an hour. The salesman leaped to safety; he followed suit and so suffered only a skinned knee. But he was close enough to see the grand and mournful splash his car made in the muddy water.

The shore-coming crew of a tramp steamer cursed him; and as he stood watching the spreading ripples a hand fell on his shoulder. He had been arrested for speeding.

After paying street car fare for himself and the optimistic salesman he had ten dollars and one cent. His fine for speeding was ten dollars.

He stood for a moment stupidly staring at [the] blank door of the station. In his hand was something round and hard; he closed his fingers on it and raised it from his pocket. In his hand was a penny—a copper cent.

He threw it into the mud of the gutter and walked on up the street, his round, fatuous face smug with self-esteem. Perhaps people would think he was a racing man, with a roll on his hip would choke an ox.

May 24, 1925

Sunset

Black Desperado Slain

The negro who has terrorized this locality for two days, killing three men, two whites and a negro, was killed last night with machine gun fire by a detachment of the —th Regiment, State National Guard. The troopers set up their gun before the copse in which the black was hiding and when there was no reply to their fire, Captain Wallace entered the place and found the negro dead. No reason has been ascertained for the black's running amuck, though it is believed he was insane. He has not been identified.

—The Clarion-Eagle.

HE CAME part of the way on or in or beneath freight cars, but mostly he walked. It took him two days to come from Carrollton avenue to Canal street, because he was afraid of the traffic; and on Canal street at last, carrying his shotgun and his bundle, he stood frightened and dazed. Pushed

and shoved, ridiculed by his own race and cursed
by policemen, he did not know what to do save
that he must cross the street.

So at last, taking his courage in both hands
and shutting his eyes, he dashed blindly across in
the middle of the block. Cars were about him, a
taxi driver screamed horrid imprecations at him,
but, clutching his gun and bundle, he made it.
And then a kind white man directed him to the
river which he sought.

And here was a boat, all tied up to the bank,
waiting for him. In climbing down a pile and
leaping six feet of water to get on it, he nearly
lost his gun; and then another white man, cursing,
drove him from the boat.

"But, cap'n," he protested, "I jest wants to go
to Af'ica. I kin pay my way."

"Africa, hell," said the white man. "Get to
hell off this boat. If you ever try to get on here
again that way I'll shoot you. Get on up yonder
and get a ticket, if you want to ride."

"Yes, suh. 'Scuse me, cap'n."

"What?" repeated the ticket seller, in amazement.

"Lemme have a ticket to Af'ica, please um."

"Do you mean Algiers?"

"No'm; Af'ica."

"Do you want a ferry ticket?"

"Yassum, I expec' so: so I kin ride dat boat
waitin' yonder."

"Come on, come on, up there," said a voice from the waiting queue behind him, so he took his ticket and was hustled through the gate and was once more on board the ferry.

To his surprise the boat, instead of going down the river, in which direction he vaguely supposed Africa to be, held straight across the stream, and he was herded ashore like a sheep. Clinging to his gun he stared about him helplessly. At last he diffidently approached a policeman.

"Cap'n, suh, is dis Af'ica?"

"Huh?" said the startled officer.

"Ah'm tryin' to get to Af'ica, please suh. Is dis de right way?"

"Africa, hell," said this white man, just as the steamboat man had done. "Look here, what are you up to?"

"Ah wants to go back home, whar de preacher say us come fum."

"Where do you live, nigger?"

"Back up yonder ways, in de country."

"What town?"

"Ain't no town, suh, 'ceptin' Mist' Bob and de fambly and his niggers."

"Mississippi or Louisana?"

"Yessuh, I 'speck so."

"Well, lemme tell you something. You go back there on the first train you can catch. This ain't no place for you."

"But, cap'n, I wants to go to Af'ica."

"You forget about Africa, and go buy yourself the longest railroad ticket you can, do you hear?"

"But, cap'n—"

"Beat it, now. Do you want me to take you up?"

At the foot of Canal street again, he looked about him in perplexity. How did one get to Africa? He was hustled and shoved this way and that, and he allowed destiny to carry him along the river front. Here was another boat tied up to the wharf, with niggers carrying things up a plank and dumping them down upon the floor. A coatless white man was evident, loudly.

Niggers pushing trucks rattled and banged, singing, about him. He was still thrust around, leaping from the path of one truck only to find another bearing down upon him. "Look out, black man!"

Suddenly the boss whirled upon him.

"What in hell are you doing? Grab aholt of something there, or get off this job. I don't have no spectators on this job at all. You hear me."

"Yas suh, cap'n," he returned equably; and soon he was throwing sacks onto a truck. His blood warmed with activity, he began to sweat and to sing. This was where he was at home—for the first time in how long? He had forgotten. "Af'ica, where is you?" he said.

Quitting time: the sun hung redly in the west and the long shadows were still and flat, waiting for dark. The spinning golden motes spun slower in the last sunlight; and the other hands gathered up coats and lunch pails and moved away toward the flashing street lights, and supper. He picked up his gun and bundle and went aboard the boat.

Among soft, bulky sacks he lay down to munch the loaf of bread he had bought. Darkness came down completely, the lapping of water against the hull and the pungently sweet smell of the sacked grain soon put him to sleep.

Motion waked him, a smooth lift and fall and a steady drumming of engines. Light was about him and he lay in a dullness of comfort, not even thinking. Then he found that he was hungry, and wondering mildly where he was, he got up.

As soon as he appeared on deck another mad white man fell upon him.

"Ah wants to go to Af'ica, cap'n," he protested, "when I holp dem niggers loadin' yestiddy Ah thought us was all goin' on dis boat."

The white man bore him down with tides of profanity. "God in heaven, you niggers will drive me crazy. Don't you know where this boat is going? It's going to Natchez."

"Dat suit me all right, jes' so she pass Af'ica. You jes' tell me when we gits dar and if she don't stop I kin jump off and swim to de bank."

The man looked at him for a long minute quite in amazement.

"En don't worry about de fare neither, suh," his passenger hastened to reassure him. "I got money: I kin pay it."

"How much you got?"

"Plenty, cap'n," he replied grandly, digging in his overalls. His outthrust hand held four silver dollars, and some smaller coins. The white man took the four dollars.

"Well, I'll take you as far as Africa for this. And you get on up there and help them niggers shift cargo until we get there."

"Yas suh!" he said with alacrity. He paused again. "But you'll sho' tell me at de right station, won't you, cap'n?"

"Yeh, sure. But beat it now, and help them other boys. G'on, now."

He helped the other boys while they passed under the perfect day from one shimmering reach of the river to another; and again the sun hung redly in the west. Bells rang somewhere and the boat sheered in toward the shore. More bells, the boat lost speed and nosed easily into the mud beneath a row of barrels. The white cap'n, the mad one, leaned down from the front porch above his head.

"All right, Jack," he roared, "here you are. Help put them barrels on board, and Africa is about a mile across them fields yonder."

He stood to watch the boat draw away from the shore, trailing black smoke from its tall funnels across the evening; then he shouldered his gun and struck inland. He had not gone far when he thought

of the lions and bears he would probably meet, so
he stopped and loaded his gun.

After walking until all the light was gone and
the Dipper swung majestically down the west, he
knew that he must be well into Africa, and that it
was time to eat and sleep again. To eat he could not,
so he decided to find a safe place to sleep. Tomorrow
he could probably kill a rabbit. He suddenly found
a fence beside him; across it loomed something that
might be a haystack. He climbed the fence and
something rose horribly from almost under his
feet.

He knew stark and terrible fear. His gun leaped
to his shoulder and roared and flamed in the darkness, and the lion or whatever it was plunged bellowing away into the night. He could feel sweat
cold as copper pieces on his face and he ran toward
the haystack and clawed madly at it, trying to
climb it. His fear grew with his futile efforts, then
cooled away, allowing him to mount the slippery
thing. Once on top he felt safe, but he was cautious
to place the shotgun close to his hand as he lay on
his belly staring into the night. The thing he had
shot was quiet now, but the night was filled with
sound.

A light came twinkling along the ground and
soon he could see legs criss-crossing it, and he heard
voices in a language he could not understand. Sav-
ages, he thought, folks that eat you; and he

crouched lower in his straw. The light and the voices passed on in the direction the beast he had shot had taken; soon the light stopped beside a blotched thing that swelled up from the ground, and the voices rose in imprecation.

"Gentlemen!" he breathed. "I mus' a shot dem folks' own private lion."

But a lion was a lion. And so he lay hidden while the light moved on away and was lost at last, and the stars swung over him, and he slept.

He was shaken into wakefulness. He threw an arm across his eyes. That strange language was in his ears again and he opened his eyes to see a small dark-skinned man kneeling over him with a pistol. The language he could not understand, but the language the pistol talked he could.

They are going to eat me! he thought. His leg gathered and sickled, the man toppled backward toward the ground, and as an animal leaps he flung himself bodily earthward. A pistol went off and something slapped him dully high in the shoulder. He replied, and a man flopped to the ground. He leaped to his feet and ran, while bullets whined past him. The fence was before him: he turned to follow it, seeking a gate.

His left arm was warm and wet, and there at the turn of the fence was a gate. The shooting behind him continued, he clutched his own gun as he saw a running figure, trying to cut him off at the gate. As they drew together he saw that this one was a mem-

ber of his own race. "Out de way, nigger," he
gasped at the other's waving arms; and he saw the
expression of ludicrous amazement on the man's
face as his gun crashed again.

His breath came in gulping lungsful. He must
stop. Here was a ditch, and a long embankment.
Just ahead, where another embankment intersected
it, was a small copse. Into this he plunged, con-
cealed, and lay on his back, panting. His heaving
lungs at last breathed easier. Then he discovered
the wound in his shoulder. He looked at his blood
in surprise. "Now when you suppose dat happen?"
he thought. "Whew! Dese Af'ikins shoots niggers
jes' like white folks does."

He bound it crudely, then took stock of the situa-
tion. He had shelter, and that was all. There were
still eighteen shells left. And he would need them:
there was already one man about two hundred yards
away, holding a rifle and watching his thicket.
"Don't ack like he gwine bother me right soon," he
decided. "I'll jes' rest here twell dark, and den I'm
gwine back to Mist' Bob. Af'ica sho' ain't no place
fer civilized folks—steppin' on lions, and bein' shot,
and havin' to shoot folks yo'self. But I guess dese
Af'icans is used to it."

His shoulder began to throb dully. He twisted
and turned in his mounting fever. How thirsty he
was! He had been hungry, but now he was only
thirsty, and he thought of the cool brown creek at
home, and the cold spring in the wood lot. He raised

his sweating face, and saw the watchman had drawn closer in. He raised his gun, aiming the best he could with one hand, and fired. The watchman fell backward, leaped to his feet and ran dodging beyond range. "Jes' to skeer you," he muttered.

Things were beginning to look funny, and his shoulder hurt dreadfully. He dozed a moment and thought he was at home again; he waked to pain and dozed again. Dozing and waking, he passed the long day, crawling at intervals to sip the muddy, stinking water in the ditch. At last he waked to night, and lanterns and fires, and men walking in the firelight and talking.

He had dragged himself down the bank for water, and as he returned an automobile's lights were suddenly turned full on him. A voice screamed, and bullets whipped about him. He plunged back to his copse and fired blindly at the lights. A man shrieked and bullets ripped and tore at the thicket: the limbs were whipped as by a gale, tortured against the sky. He was seared as with hot irons, and he lowered his head, pressing his face into the muddy earth.

The firing suddenly ceased; the silence literally dragged him from the regions of oblivion. He thrust his gun forward, waiting. At last the darkness detached itself and became two things; and in the flash of his point-blank explosion he saw two men crouching. One of them fired a pistol almost in his face, and fled.

Again it was dawn. The sun rose, became hot, and marched above his head. He was at home, working in the fields; he was asleep, fighting his way from out a nightmare; he was a child again—no, he was a bird, a big one like a buzzard, drawing endless black circles on a blue sky.

Again the sun sank. The west was like blood: it was his own blood painted onto a wall. Supper in the pot, and night where there were no fires and people moving around them, and then all stopping as though they were waiting for something to happen.

He raised his face from the mud and looked at the circle of fires about him. It looked as though everybody had gathered at one place, directly in front of him, all watching or waiting for something. Let them wait: tomorrow he'll be at home, with Mr. Bob to curse him in his gentle voice, and regular folks to work and laugh and talk with.

Here was a wind coming up: the branches and bushes about him whipped suddenly to a gale fiercer than any yet; flattened and screamed, and melted away under it. And he, too, was a tree caught in that same wind: he felt the dull blows of it, and the rivening of himself into tattered and broken leaves.

The gale died away, and all broken things were still. His black, kind, dull, once-cheerful face was turned up to the sky and the cold, cold stars. Africa or Louisiana: what care they?

May 31, 1925

The Kid Learns

COMPETITION IS EVERYWHERE: competition makes the world go round. Not love, as some say. Who would want a woman nobody else wanted? Not me. And not you. And not Johnny. Same way about money. If nobody wanted the stuff, it wouldn't be worth fighting for. But more than this is being good in your own line, whether it is selling aluminum or ladies' underwear or running whiskey, or what. Be good, or die.

"Listen," said Johnny, tilted back against the wall in his chair, "a man ain't only good in our business because he'd get his otherwise, he's good because he wants to be a little better than the best, see?"

"Sure," said his friend Otto, sitting beside him, not moving.

"Anybody can keep from getting bumped off. All you gotta do is get took on a street gang or as a soda squirt. What counts is being good as you

can—being good as any of 'em. Getting yours or
not getting yours just shows how good you are or
how good you ought to of been.''

"Sure," agreed his friend Otto, tilting forward
his brief derby and spitting.

"Listen, I ain't got nothing against the Wop,
see; but he sets hisself up as being good and I sets
myself up as being good, and some day we got to
prove between us which is the best."

"Yeh," said Otto, rolling a slender cigarette and
flicking a match on his thumb nail, "but take your
time. You're young, see; and he's an old head at
this. Take your time. Get some age onto you and
I'm playing you on the nose at any odds. They
wasn't no one ever done a better job in town than
the way you taken that stuff away from him last
week, but get some age onto you before you brace
him, see? I'm for you: you know damn well."

"Sure," said Johnny in his turn, "I ain't no
fool. Gimme five years, though, and it'll be Johnny
Gray, with not even the bulls to remember the Wop.
Five years, see?"

"That's the kid. They ain't nothing to com-
plain, the way we done lately. Let her ride as she
lays, and when the time comes we'll clean 'em all."

"And he's right," thought Johnny, walking
down the street. "Take time, and get yourself
good. They ain't nobody good from the jump:
you got to learn to be good. I ain't no fool, I got

sense enough to lay off the Wop until the time
comes. And when it does—good-night."

He looked up and his entrails became briefly
cold—not with fear, but with the passionate knowledge of what was some day to be. Here was the Wop
in an identical belted coat and Johnny felt a sharp
envy in spite of himself. They passed; Johnny nodded, but the other only jerked a casual, patronizing
finger at him. Too proud to look back, he could see
in his mind the swagger of the other's revealed
shoulders and the suggestion of a bulge over his
hip. Some day! Johnny swore beneath his breath,
and he ached for that day.

Then he saw her.

Down the street she came, swinging her flat
young body with all the awkward grace of youth,
swinging her thin young arms; beneath her hat he
saw hair neither brown nor gold, and gray eyes.
Clean as a colt she swung past him, and turning to
follow her with his eyes and all the vague longing
of his own youth, he saw the Wop step gracefully
out and accost her.

Saw her recoil, and saw the Wop put his hand
on her arm. And Johnny knew that that thing he
had wanted to wait for until his goodness was better
had already come. The Wop had prisoned both her
arms when he thrust between them, but he released
his grasp in sheer surprise on recognizing Johnny.

"Beat it," commanded Johnny coldly.

"Why, you poor fish, whatayou mean? You talking to me?"

"Beat it, I said," Johnny repeated.

"You little —— —— ——," and the older man's eyes grew suddenly red, like a rat's. "Don't you know who I am?" He thrust Johnny suddenly aside and again grasped the girl's arm. The back of her hand was pressed against her mouth and she was immovable with fear. When he touched her she screamed, Johnny leaped and struck the Wop on his unguarded jaw, and she fled down the street, wailing. Johnny's pistol was out and he stood over the felled man as Otto ran up.

"My God!" Otto shouted, "you've done it now!" He dragged a weighted bit of leather from his pocket. "I don't dast croak him here. I'll put him out good, and you beat it, get out of town, quick!" He tapped the still groggy man lightly and ran. "Beat it quick, for God's sake!" he cried over his shoulder. But Johnny had already gone after the girl, and a policeman, running heavily, appeared.

Before a darkened alleyway he overtook her. She had stopped, leaning against the wall with her face in the crook of her arm, gasping and crying. When he touched her she screamed again, whirling and falling. He caught and supported her.

"It ain't him, it's me," he told her obscurely. "There, there; it's all right. I laid him out."

She clung to him, sobbing; and poor Johnny

gazed about him, trapped. Cheest, what did you do with a weeping girl?

"Now, now, baby," he repeated, patting her back awkwardly, as you would a dog's, "it's all right. He won't bother you. Tell me where you live, and I'll take you home."

"O-o-o-oh, he sc-scared me s-o," she wailed, clinging to him. Poor kid, she didn't know that he was the one to be scared, that his was the life that was about to take a dark and unknown corner, for better or worse, only the gods knew. There is still time to get out of town, though, caution told him. Otto is right; he knows best. Leave her and beat it, you fool! Leave her, and him back yonder? Youth replied. Not by your grandmother's false teeth, I won't.

He felt her pliant young body shudder with fear and her choked weeping.

"There, there, kid," he repeated inanely. He didn't know what to say to 'em, even. But he must get her away from here. The Wop would be about recovering now, and he'd be looking for him. He held her closer and her trembling gradually died away; and looking about him he almost shouted with relief. Here was old Ryan the cop's house, that had known him boy and lad for fifteen years. The very place.

"Why, say, here's the very place. Mrs. Ryan knows me, she'll look after you until I come back for you."

She clasped him sharply in her thin arms. "No, no, don't leave me! I'm so scared!"

"Why, just for a minute, honey," he reassured her, "just until I find where he went, see? We don't wanta stumble on him again."

"No, no, no, he'll hurt you!" Her wet salty face was against his. "You mustn't! You mustn't!"

"Sure, just a while, baby. I won't be no time." She moaned against Johnny's face and he kissed her cold mouth, and it was as though dawn had come among the trees where the birds were singing. They looked at each other a moment.

"Must you?" she said in a changed voice, and she allowed herself to be led to the dark door; and they clung to each other until footsteps came along the passage within the house. She put her arms around Johnny's neck again.

"Hurry back," she whispered, "and oh, be careful. I'm so afraid!"

"Baby!"

"Sweetheart!"

The door opened upon Mrs. Ryan, there was a brief explanation, and with her damp kiss yet on his face, Johnny ducked quickly from the alleyway.

Here were flying remote stars above, but below were flashing lights and paved streets, and all the city smells that he loved. He could go away for a while, and then come back, and things—lights and streets and smells—would be the same. "No!" he swore. "I've got a girl now. I ruther be bumped off than have her know I run." But ah, if this could have been put off a while! How sweet she is! Is this love, I wonder? he thought, or is it being afraid, makes me want to run back to her and risk letting things work themselves out instead of doing it myself? Anyway, I done it for her: I wasn't double-crossing the boys. I had to do it: anyone can see that.

"Well, I ain't as good as I wanted, but I can be as good as I can." He looked again at the flying stars, his pistol loose in his pocket, and smelled again the smells of food and gasoline that he loved; and one stepped quickly from out a doorway.

Why, say, here she was again beside him, with her young body all shining and her hair that wasn't brown and wasn't gold and her eyes the color of sleep; but she was somehow different at the same time.

"Mary?" said Johnny, tentatively.

"Little sister Death," corrected the shining one, taking his hand.

July 26, 1925

The Liar

FOUR MEN SAT COMFORTABLY on the porch of Gibson's store, facing the railroad tracks and two nondescript yellow buildings. The two buildings belonged to the railroad company, hence they were tidy in an impersonal way, and were painted the same prodigious yellow. The store, not belonging to the railroad company, was not painted. It squatted stolidly against a rising hill, so that the proprietor could sit at ease, spitting into the valley, and watch the smoke-heralded passing of casual trains. The store and the proprietor resembled each other, slovenly and comfortable; and it was seldom that the owner's was the only chair tilted against the wall, and his the only shavings littering the floor.

Today he had four guests. Two of these had ridden in from the hills for trivial necessities, the other two had descended from the morning's local freight; and they sat in easy amity, watching the smoke from the locomotive dwindle away down the valley.

"Who's that feller, coming up from the deepo?" spoke one at last. The others followed his gaze and the stranger mounted the path from the station under their steady provincial stare. He was roughly dressed—a battered felt hat, a coarse blue cloth jacket and corduroy trousers—a costume identical with that of at least one of the watchers.

"Never seen him before. He don't live here-abouts, that I know of," murmured the proprietor. "Any of you boys know him?"

They shook their heads. "Might be one of them hill fellers. They stays back yonder all the year round, some of 'em ain't never been out." The speaker, a smallish man with a large round bald head and a long saturine face in which his two bleached eyes were innocent and keen—like a depraved priest—continued: "Feller over to Mitchell says one of 'em brung his whole family into town one day last month to let 'em see a train. Train blowed, and his wife and six-seven children started milling round kind of nervous; but when she come in sight around the bend the whole bunch broke for the woods.

"Old man Mitchell himself had drove down fer his paper, and them hill folks run right spang over his outfit: tore his buggy all to pieces and scart his hoss so bad it took 'em till next day noon to catch him. Yes, sir, heard 'em whooping and hollering all

night, trying to head that hoss into something with
a fence around it. They say he run right through
old Mis' Harmon's house—" The narrator broke
down over his own invention. His audience laughed
too, enjoying the humor, but tolerantly, as one
laughs at a child. His fabling was well known. And
though like all peoples who live close to the soil,
they were by nature veracious, they condoned his
unlimited imagination for the sake of the humor he
achieved and which they understood.

The laughter ceased, for the newcomer was near.
He mounted the shaky steps and stood among them,
a dark-favored man. "Morning, gentlemen," he
greeted them without enthusiasm.

The proprietor, as host, returned his greeting.
The others muttered something, anything, as was
the custom. The stranger entered the store and the
owner rose reluctantly and luxuriously to follow
him.

"Say," spoke the raconteur, "ever notice how
spry Will is for trade? See him jump up when a
customer comes in, and nigh tromps his heels off
herding him inside? Minds me of the time—"

"Shet up, Ek," another told him equably. "You
already told one lie this morning. Give a man time
to smoke a pipe betwixt 'em, leastways. Mebbe that
stranger'd like to hear ye. And Will'd hate to miss
it, too." The others guffawed, and spat.

Gibson and his customer returned; the proprietor sank with a sigh into his chair and the other,

bearing a piece of cheese and a paper sack of crackers, lowered himself onto the top step, his back against a post, partly facing them. He began his meal while they stared at him, gravely and without offense, as children, and all whose desires and satisfactions are simple, can.

"Say, Will," said one after a while, "you come near missing one of Ek's yarns. Us fellers stopped him, though. Now, Ek, you kin go ahead."

"Lissen," said the one called Ek, readily, "all you boys think that ever' time I open my mouth it's to do a little blanket stretching, but lemme tell you something cur'ous that reely happened. 'Twas like this—"

He was interrupted. "H'y, Will, git out yer hoss medicine: Ek's took sick."

"Musta had a stroke. We kept telling him ter stay outen them sunny fields."

"Yes, sir; shows what work'll do fer you."

"No, boys, it's that licker them Simpson boys makes: Makes a man tell the truth all the time. Sho' better keep it outen the courts, or ever'body'll be in jail."

Ek had vainly striven to surmount the merriment. "You fellers don't know nothing," he roared. "Feller comes trying to tell you the truth—" They shouted him down again, and Will Gibson summed the matter up.

"Why, Ek, we ain't doubting your ability to tell the truth when it's necessary, like in court or

meeting house; but they ain't no truth ever happened as entertaining as your natural talk, hey
boys? He's better'n a piece in the theayter, ain't he,
fellers?"

The others assented loudly, but Ek refused to
be mollified. He sat in offended dignity. The others
chuckled at intervals, but at last the merriment was
gone and there was no sound save the stranger's
methodical crunching. He, seemingly, had taken no
part in the laughter. Far up the valley a train whistled; echo took the sound and toyed with it, then
let it fade back into silence.

But silence was unbearable to Ek. At last it
overcame his outraged dignity. "Say," he went
easily into narrative, "lemme tell you something
cur'ous that reely happened to me yest'day. I was
over to Mitchell yest'day waiting for the early local,
when I meets up with Ken Rogers, the sheriff. We
passed the time of day and he says to me, what am
I doing today, and I tells him I aim to ride No. 12
over home. Then he says he's looking for somebody
like me, asking me wasn't I raised in the hills. I
tells him I was, and how when I turned twenty-one,
paw decided I had ought to wear shoes. I hadn't
never worn no shoes, and was young and skittish as
a colt in them days.

"Well, sir, you may believe it or not, but when
they come to my pallet that morning with them new
shoes, I up and lit out of there in my shirt tail
and took to the woods. Paw sent word around to

the neighbors and they organized a hunt same as a bear hunt, with axes and ropes and dogs. No guns, though; paw held that to shoot me would be a waste of manpower, as I could stand up to a day's work with any of 'em.

"Well, sir, it took 'em two days to git me, and they only got me then when them big man-eating hounds of Lem Haley's put me up a tree in Big Sandy bottom, twenty miles from home. And mebbe you won't believe it, but it took paw and three strong men to put them shoes on me." He led the laughter himself, which the stranger joined. "Yes, sir; them was the days. But lemme see, I kind of got off the track. Where was I? Oh, yes. Well, the sheriff he says to me can't I go back in the hills a ways with him. And I says, well, I dunno; I got some business in Sidon to tend to today—"

"Same business you're tending to now, I reckon?" interrupted one of his audience. "Got to git back where folks believe him when he says he's telling the truth."

"Now, look-a-here," began the affronted narrator, when the proprietor interfered. "Hush up, you Lafe; let him finish his tale. G'on, Ek, won't nobody bother you again."

Ek looked at him in gratitude and resumed. "Well, listen. The sheriff, he says to me, he needs a man that knows them hill folks to go in with him. Been some trouble of some kind and he wants to clear it up. But them hill people is so leary that

they's liable to shoot first, before a man kin state
his point. So he wants I should go along with him
and kind of mollify 'em, you might say, promising
to get me back in time to catch the evening train.
Well, they ain't nothing I couldn't put off a day
or so, so I goes with him. He's got his car all ready
and a deppity waiting, so we piles in and lit out.

"It was as putty a day as I ever see and we was
having a good time, laughing and talking back and
forth—"

Lafe interrupted again: "Must of been, with a
set of fellers't never heard your lies before."

"Be quiet, Lafe," Gibson commanded peremp-
torily.

"—and first thing I knew, we come to a place
where the road played out altogether. 'Have to
walk from here on,' sheriff says, so we runs the car
off the road a ways, and struck out afoot. Well, sir,
I was born and raised in them hills, but I never seen
that stretch where we was before—all ridges, and
gullies where you could sling a hoss off and lose him.
Finally the sheriff says to me: 'Ek,' he says, 'place
we're heading for is jest across that ridge. You go
on over to the house, and tell Mrs. Starnes who you
are; and Tim and me'll go around yonder way.
Probably catch Joe in his lower field. We'll meet
you at the house. Might ask Mis' Starnes if she kin
git us a little snack ready.'

" 'All right, sheriff,' I says, 'but I don't know
nobody through here.'

" 'That's all right,' sheriff says, 'jest go up to the house and tell her me and Joe and Tim'll be 'long soon.' And him and Tim started on around the ridge, and I took the route he give me. Well, sir, I moseyed on up to the top of the ridge, and sho' 'nough, there was a house and a barn setting in the next valley. It didn't look like much of a farm and I just decided them Starneses was average shif'less hill folks. There was a lot of rocks on the ridge where I was, and just as I was thinking what a good place for snakes it was and starting on down to'rds the house—bzzzrrr! went something right behind me. Gentlemen, I jumped twenty foot and lit grabbing rocks. When I had throwed a couple the rattler was gone into a hole; and then I seen three others laying with their heads mashed, and I knowed I must of stumbled into a regular den of 'em. They hadn't been dead long, and from the sample I'd had I knowed how mad the others must be, so I lit a shuck out of there. But I wasn't far from the feller had killed them three, but just how close I never learnt till later.

"I dropped on down through the brush, coming to the house from behind. Down the hill from the barn and between me and the house was a spring in a rocky gully. The spring was railed off from cattle. There was gullies and rocks ever'where: I never seen such pore, rocky land—sink holes full of rocks and narrer as wells. I had to jump 'em like a goat.

"I was about half-way down the hill when I seen a feller moving down at the spring. I hadn't seen him before. He jest wasn't there when I looked once, but there he was when I looked again, rising up by the spring. He had a wooden box under his arm. I never knowed where he come from.

"Knowing how skittish them hill folks are, I was jest about to sing out when he put his finger in his mouth and whistled. I thought mebbe he was calling his dog, and I was thinking to myself it was a sorry dog that never suspicioned me when I was this close, when a woman come to the back door of the house. She stood there a minute, shading her eyes and looking all around at the ridges, but she never did look to'rds the spring. Then she stepped out, toting something in her hand, and started fer the spring on the run. Then I could see she had her Sunday hat on, and that the thing in her hand was a carpetbag. Fellers, she jest flew down that hill.

" 'Uh, uh,' thinks I to myself, 'they's something going on here that I don't know about, and that Starnes don't know nothing about, neither.' The sheriff seemed mighty certain he wouldn't be to home, and I never seen a man and wife go to all that trouble to go anywheres.

"Well, sir, they met at the spring. The feller had set his little box down careful, and they was clamped together like two sheep in a storm, and was a-kissing. 'Uh, uh!' thinks I, 'here's something else me and Starnes don't know nothing about, and what'd make him itch if he did.' I was higher up than them two, and I taken a look around fer sheriff and Tim, and I seen a lone feller coming down the valley. They couldn't see him a tall, but jest when I seen him, he spied them. He stopped a minute like he was studying, then he come on, not hiding exactly, but walking careful.

"Meanwhile, them two at the spring was bent over the feller's little box, and I seen her jump back and kind of squeal. Well, sir, things was getting cur'ouser and cur'ouser ever' minute, and I was a-wishing and a-griping for sheriff and Tim to git there. 'If sheriff's wanting something to clear up,' I thinks to myself, 'I got it here waiting fer him.' And about then things begun to pop.

"Them two at the spring looked up all on a sudden. They had either seen or heard the other feller; so he walked in bold as you please. The woman she kind of comes behind the first feller; then she drops her bag and makes a bee-line fer the other one, the feller that jest come up, and tries to grab him round the neck. He flings her off and she fell flat, but jumped up and tried to grab him again.

"Well, sir, she kep' on trying to hold his arm and he kep' on a-flinging her off, all the time walking not fast but steady to'rds number one. Finally she sees she can't stop 'em, so she backed off with her hands kind of against her side, and I can see she is scared most to death. Them two fellers is about a yard apart, when number two hauled off

and knocked the other one clean into the spring.
He jumped up right away and grabbed up a
rail from the fence that kep' cattle out of the
spring. The woman hollered and grabbed at number two again, and while he was shaking her loose,
number one ups and hits him over the head with
his rail, and he dropped like a ox. Them hill folks
has got hard heads, but it seemed to me I could
hear that feller's skull bust. Leastways, he never
moved again. The woman backed off, clamping
her head betwixt her hands; and the feller watched
him awhile, then throwed away his rail.

"Well, sir, you could of knocked me down with
a straw. There I was, watching murder, skeered to
move, and no sign of sheriff and Tim. I've got
along fine without no law officers, but I sho' needed
one then." Ek stopped, with consummate art, and
gazed about on his hearers. Their eyes were enraptured on his face, the hot black gaze of the stranger
seemed like a blade spitting him against the wall,
like a pinned moth. The train whistled again, un-
heard.

"Go on, go on," breathed Gibson.

He drew his gaze from the stranger's by an effort of will, and found that the pleasant May
morning was suddenly chill. For some reason he did
not want to continue.

"Well, sir, I didn't know whether the feller
would finish his job right then or not; seemed like
he didn't know himself. And all the time the woman

was like she was took by a spell. Finally he walked
over and picked the unconscious feller up, and carried him about fifteen foot down the gulley, then
dumped him like a sack of meal into one of them
narrow sink holes. And all the time the woman was
watching him like she was turned to stone." The
train whistled again and the locomotive came in
sight, but not one turned his eyes from the narrator's face.

"Seemed like he had decided what to do now.
He run back to'rds where the woman was, and I
thinks, my God, he's going to kill her, too. But no,
he's just after his box. He grabs it up and come
back to where he had throwed the other feller. Well,
sir, if I could have been cur'ous over anything right
then, I would have been cur'ous over what he was
a-doing now. But as it was, I was past thinking:
jest goggle-eyed, like a fish when you jerk him out
the water.

"And all the time this feller is fiddling with his
box, standing on the edge of that sink hole. All on a
sudden he helt it out from him, shaking it over the
hole. Finally something all knotted and shiny like
a big watch chain fell out of it and dropped, shining and twisting, into the place where the other feller was.

"Then I knowed who'd killed them rattlers."
"My God," said someone.
"Yes, sir. They'd planned to fix that there snake

where number two'd stumble on it when he come in, only he come too soon for 'em."

"My God!" repeated the voice, then the one called Lafe screamed:

"Look out!"

A pistol said whow, the sound slammed against the front of the store and roared across the porch. Ek rolled from his chair and thumped on the floor, tried to rise, and fell again. Lafe sprang erect, but the others sat in reft and silent amaze, watching the stranger leaping down the path toward the track and the passing train; saw him recklessly grasp a car ladder and, shaving death by inches, scramble aboard.

* *

Later, when the doctor had ridden ten miles, dressed Ek's shoulder, cursed him for a fool, and gone, the four of them took him to task.

"Well, Ek, I guess you learnt your lesson. You'll know better than tell the truth again."

"Ain't it the beatingest thing? Here's a man lied his way through life fer forty years and never got a scratch, then sets out to tell the truth fer once in his life, and gets shot."

"But what was your point," Will Gibson reiterated, "in telling your fool yarn right in front of the feller that did it? Didn't you know him again?"

Ek turned his fever exasperated face to them.

"I tell you that it was all a lie, ever last word of it. I wasn't nowhere near Mitchell yest'day."

They shook their heads at his obstinacy; then Gibson, seeing that they were increasing the patient's fever, drove them out. The last to go, he turned at the door for a parting shot.

"I don't know whether you were lying, or were telling the truth, but either way, you must get a whole lot of satisfaction out of this. If you were lying, you ought to be shot for telling one so prob'le that it reely happened somewhere; and if you were telling the truth, you ought to be shot for having no better sense than to blab it out in front of the man that done the killing. Either way, if you ain't learnt a lesson, I have. And this is, don't talk at all lessen you have to, and when you got to talk, tell the truth."

"Aw, get out of here," snarled Ek. And convicted of both truthfulness and stupidity, he turned his face bitterly to the wall, knowing that his veracity as a liar was gone forever.

August 16, 1925

Episode

EVERY DAY AT NOON they pass. He in a brushed suit and a gray hat, never collarless nor tieless, she in a neat cotton print dress and a sunbonnet. I have seen her any number of times, sitting and rocking upon wooden porches before the crude, shabby cottages among my own hills in Mississippi.

They are at least sixty. He is blind and his gait is halting and brittle. Talking in a steady stream, gesturing with her knotty hand, she leads him daily to the cathedral to beg; at sunset she returns for him and takes him home. I had not seen her face until Spratling from the balcony called to her. She looked to both sides and then behind her without discovering us. At Spratling's second call she looked up.

Her face is brown, and timeless and merry as a gnome's and toothless: her nose and chin know each other.

"Are you in a hurry?" he asked.

"Why?" she replied brightly.

"I'd like to sketch you."

She watched his face keenly, not comprehending.

"I'd like to make a picture of you," he explained.

"Come down," she replied promptly, smiling. She spoke to the man with her and he obediently tried to sit down upon the narrow concrete base of the garden fence. He fell heavily and a passer-by helped her raise him to his feet. I left Spratling feverishly seeking a pencil and descended with a chair for him, and I saw that she was actually trembling—not with age, but with pleased vanity.

"Assiz, Joe," she ordered, and he sat down, his sightless face filled with that remote godlike calm known only to the blind. Spratling with his sketch pad appeared. She took her place beside the seated man with her hand on his shoulder: one knew immediately that they had been photographed so on their wedding day.

She was a bride again; with that ability for fine fabling which death alone can rob us of, she was once more dressed in silk (or its equivalent) and jewels, a wreath and a veil, and probably a bouquet. She was a bride again, young and fair, with her trembling hand on young Joe's shoulder; Joe beside her was once more something to shake her heart with dread and adoration and vanity— something to be a little frightened of.

A casual passer-by felt it and stopped to look at them. Even blind Joe felt it through her hand on his shoulder. Her dream clothed him, too, in

188

youth and pride; he too assumed that fixed and
impossible attitude of the male and his bride being
photographed in the year 1880.

"No, no," Spratling told her, "not like that."
Her face fell. "Turn toward him, look at him,"
he added quickly.

She obeyed, still facing us.

"Turn your head too; look at him."

"But you can't see my face then," she objected.

"Yes, I can. Besides, I'll draw your face later."

Appeased, her smile broke her face into a
million tiny wrinkles, like an etching, and she took
the position he wanted.

At once she became maternal. She was no longer
a bride; she had been married long enough to know
that Joe was not anything to be either loved or
feared very passionately, but on the contrary he
was something to be a little disparaging of; that
after all he was only a large, blundering child.
(You knew she had borne children by now—perhaps lost one.) But he was hers and another would
be as bad probably, so she would make the best
of it, remembering other days.

And Joe, again taking her mood through her
hand on his shoulder, was no longer the dominat-
ing male. And he too, remembering other days
when he had come to her for comfort, took her
new dream. His arrogance dissolved from him
and he sat quiet under her touch, helpless yet
needing no help, sightless and calm as a god
who has seen both life and death and found noth-

ing of particular importance in either of them.

Spratling finished.

"Now the face," she reminded him quickly. And now there was something in her face that was not her face. It partook of something in time, in the race, ambiguous, enigmatic. Was she posing? I wondered, watching her. She was facing Spratling, but I don't believe her eyes saw him, nor the wall behind him. Her eyes were contemplative, yet personal—it was as if someone had whispered a sublime and colossal joke in the ear of an idol.

Spratling finished, and her face became the face of a woman of sixty, toothless and merry as a gnome's. She came over to see the sketch, taking it in her hands.

"Got any money?" Spratling asked me.

I had fifteen cents. She returned the picture without comment and took the coins.

"Thank you," she said. She touched her husband and he rose. "Thank you for the chair," she nodded and smiled at me, and I watched them move slowly down the alley, wondering what I had seen in her face—or had I seen anything at all. I turned to Spratling. "Let's see it."

He was staring at the sketch. "Hell," he said. I looked at it. And then I knew what I had seen in her face. The full-face sketch had exactly the same expression as the Mona Lisa.

Ah, women, who have but one eternal age! And that is no age.

September 20, 1925

Country Mice

MY FRIEND the bootlegger's motor car is as long as a steamboat and the color of a chocolate ice cream soda. It is trimmed with silver from stem to stern like an expensive lavatory. It is upholstered in maroon leather and attached to it, for emergencies and convenience, is every object which the ingenuity of its maker could imagine my friend ever having any possible desire for or need of. Except a coffin. It is my firm belief that on the first opportunity his motor car is going to retaliate by quite viciously obliterating him.

We were pursuing a custom of ours, an obnoxious habit which he had formed for me and which he called "airing off"; i.e., to take the shortest way out of town and then to go somewhere, anywhere, at between forty and seventy miles an hour. He never drives faster than seventy because for some reason his car will not go any faster than seventy miles an hour. I am constantly uneasy over the expectation that some day someone will show him how to make it go eighty miles an hour. And I simply cannot afford an untimely dissolution: I have my living to earn. However, I am by nature an incurable optimist; he seems to enjoy my company, and some day I hope to get a story out of him, for marvelous are the tales he so casually tells me of his early struggles trying to make label and bottle meet. And there you are.

My friend the bootlegger is consistently paradoxical. His shirt is of silk and striped viciously, and collarless; in its front is a ruby stud (genuine) the size of a small olive; looping from his belt to his pocket is a gold and platinum and yet virgin watch chain: he believes it is unlucky to carry a watch, and besides when he goes anywhere he travels by a speed indicator; he owns a gold and elegant cigarette case of fourteen net ounces displacement which, when opened, reveals a brand of cigarettes which may be purchased anywhere at fifty for twenty-five cents. But to get on.

We were, as I think I stated before, airing off. The road was straight and white as a swift unrolling ribbon, and Louisiana rushed by us in a fretful, indistinguishable green. Wind plopped at my ears and my eyelashes turned backward irritatingly, keeping me blinking. Then something happened. I noticed with surprise that the wind no longer plopped so loudly at my ears. Imagine my surprise to find that we were going only thirty-five miles an hour—practically crawling. We were approaching a small village: two rows of houses facing each other across the road.

"They'll have time to dodge after they hear you, at this speed," I shouted warningly at his ear.

"Dodge, hell," he replied. "I'm the one that's dodging." He caught my glance of inquiry and added: "Constable."

"Why, you don't mind a little thing like a hick constable, do you?" I asked in surprise. We had left the village in our dust and the speedometer began to climb.

"Lemme tell you something, brother—" he mashed his gleaming yellow shoe heavily on the throttle "—say what you want to about country cops, call 'em hicks if you want; but when you fool with one of them birds, get up early in the morning to do it, see? I know 'em. I used to think about 'em like you do, but one learned me better." He glanced at the speedometer and mashed his foot harder. She was only doing sixty-six.

"Yes?" I screamed. He stared ahead frowingly, preoccupied. His car was practically new, but I knew that he already dreamed of a car that would go seventy-five miles an hour, or even eighty. It was not seventy miles an hour he wanted, it was five miles an hour for which he pined. But such is the immortal soul of man.

At last she showed seventy and he sighed, settling down to enjoy himself. "Yes sir. You can say what you. . . . 'member when. . . . what you call a hick cop. . . ." The wind tore the words from his tongue. I leaned toward him, clutching my hat.

"I can't hear you!" I screamed diffidently. "If you'd slow down a bit. . . ."

He complied, giving me his quick Italian glance. "I couldn't hear you," I explained when we had dropped to conversational speed.

"Oh sure," he agreed with his habitual courtesy. "This come off when I was in New York. Doing a good business, making lots of jack. I was in with the big fellows, see?" He sighed again in retrospection. "Them was good times then, before them politicians ruined the liquor business. But it's shot to hell, now. No more money in it. I work like a nigger to make a living, even, now; while back in them days. . . ." He brooded briefly toward his lost alcoholic Nirvana. "But now when you got to sell it at thirty-six a case. . . .Well," he said philosophically, "they don't nothing last forever, does it? But she was sure a pretty business at one time. I remember—"

"But about this hick cop," I suggested, recalling him.

"Oh yes. Well, it was in the fall of '20 or '21, when the liquor business was so good, when you could stick 'em one-fifty and two hundred a case. Me and my brother was in the East then. And so this bird I knew comes to me and suggests that we bring a bunch of hooch into New Haven, a town up the road from New York, where they was going to have a big football game, and we'd clean up. New Haven is where one of them big colleges is, I forget the name of it—"

"Yale," I suggested.

"I guess so. Anyway, this bird I'm telling you about had been there and he knew how everything stacked up. My brother he went on up to Montreal to get the stuff lined up and ready to go, and me and the other fellow goes up to New Haven. You been to a college town, ain't you?"

I admitted that I had, and he continued:

"It was a funny town, quiet seeming, but plenty of business in my line. We never had no trouble at all getting ourselves set pretty as you'd want. Waiting for word from my brother, see. We had everything fixed for him, all the cops along the route had been fixed all right, and all he had to do was to bring them trucks right on down like he was going to a Sunday school picnic. They wasn't only one thing we had to worry about —hi-jackers. And we'd fixed him up with as pretty a gang of cutthroats as you ever seen for guards. I knew I could depend on him: honest and clever as the day is long. The day they started out he wired me at New Haven, and so we was all set.

"Well, we mixed around in New Haven and got to know some nice people and we was spending a nice week up there, knowing that everything was jake or Gus, that's my brother, would have wired us, when one night they came a long distance telephone for me.

"Yeh, it was Gus. In some jay town, I forget the name of it. They had had a run-in with some hi-jackers and had turned off the route onto another road and—bang. A hayseed cop that hadn't been fixed held 'em up. Wouldn't listen to reason, wouldn't consider nothing. Color blind, too. So Gus put up his bail and put away his roll and beat it to the telephone. Jees, I was mad. If anybody'd been listening in, I'd a got pinched sure. So me and the other bird grabbed a taxi and caught the first train.

"Well sir, we tried everything with that J. P. Showed him some real money, told him they was more—fellow, I talked to that old gray-haired —— —— —— like a brother. But it never moved him no more than one of them New England rocks; say, I'd a stood more chance buying Republican votes in front of Tammany Hall. I didn't know what to do. But this other bird he wouldn't give up. He said you couldn't tell him they wasn't no way of fixing this thing; that this country had got in a hell of a way if they could sew you up like this. Well, I told him to fly at it, that I'd give him ten bucks a case for all of it we moved. And I went to the hotel and set down so I could groan comfortable.

"I'd been there about an hour, I guess, when here comes my partner. 'Buck up,' he says, slapping me on the back. 'It's all fixed. It's going to cost us twenty-five a case to move it and we got to do it quick.'

" 'Pinch yourself,' I says, 'you're dreaming.'

" 'Dreaming yourself,' he says. 'You better be glad I got out and done something instead of setting here crying into my own vest.'

" 'All right,' I says, 'if you got the dope, spill it.' I still thought he was kidding me, see?

"But he wasn't. He had got next to the deputy that was guarding the barn where the trucks was, and they had agreed on twenty-five a case. That was pretty steep, but then we'd just shove her up a few dollars ourselves—folks don't care what they give for a case of the stuff, when they are celebrating. Only I wanted to be darn sure we wouldn't be held up again. But this deputy had fixed that, even. He knowed a fellow in Boston that had a airplane, see, and he said he knowed we could get it, though we might have to buy it. So I told him to fly at it and get his buddy here by nightfall, as we didn't have but over tomorrow before the football game was pulled off. So he said all right, he'd have him here like he said.

"Well, sure enough that night the deputy brought the airplane fellow around to see us. And they was as like as two peas: they looked exactly alike. Well sir, I look at my partner and I think for Pete's sake, and he looks at me thinking the same thing. And this deputy says, 'This is my twin brother,' like he'd just thought of it. But when we got down to business the airplane fellow was as stubborn as the J. P. had been. I ought to of knowed then, but seems like our luck was against us: we was worse than two children. What do you think he wanted for his airplane? Not to rent it to us: he couldn't see that at all. We must buy it outright or—good-night. And what you guess he wanted? One thousand dollars."

He pronounced the words with vicious unction. Then he became temporarily unprintable, tramping heavily on the throttle. My spine snapped to our speed.

"And what then?" I shrieked. He slowed down.

"What else could we do? They wasn't no other way to get the stuff there on time, and I could see in that deputy's eye that if we turned his brother down, it was all off all around. They had us, see? All we could hope for was to get our money out now. So me and my partner asked 'em to excuse us a moment while we went into the next room and talked it over.

" 'So this is the way you handle these hick officers, huh?' I says to him.

" 'At least it's better'n the way you handle 'em,' he comes back.

" 'I admit that,' I says, 'specially if you base your calculations on what it's going to cost us.'

" 'That ain't neither here nor there,' he says. 'What we've got to do is to get out the best way we can. And that is—' I seen his point right off.

" '—and that is to hi-jack that deputy for that twenty-five a case as soon as we get started.'

"So we matched, to see which one of us went with the stuff and which one stayed to fix that deputy. And I lost. What? Hell, no. I'd rather of walked in the White House and stuck up the president at his own dinner table than ride in that airplane. But I lost.

"Well, we met 'em at the barn where the trucks was. We had sent Gus on to New Haven to get everything lined up, and the deputy had a couple of men there. And we worked like dogs, putting all we could into that airplane. Finally she had as much as the fellow thought she'd carry and we was all set as soon as it got light. I stalled around so the deputy wouldn't have time to hide the jack, then I paid him what we had agreed on, and him and his brother got the airplane motor started and I called Joe off to one side and tried again to make him swap with me. When I'd look at that damn airplane and think about I was going up in it—I was all ready to call it off and let 'em have the stuff. But I got a weak stomach, anyway, specially before breakfast.

" 'Ah, come on,' Joe says. 'You wanna let 'em see you're yellow?'

" 'Let 'em see. I admit I'm yellow.'

"'Ah, brace up, brace up. Why, I wouldn't be afraid to go with him, if only I didn't have this other thing to see to.'

"'Hell,' I says, 'I'll see to that. It'll be a pleasure. You go with him.'

"But he wouldn't do it. 'It's bad luck to change your plans,' he gave as his reason.

"'I've heard your theory of bad luck lots of times,' I says, 'but that's a new one on me.'

"But by then they was calling us. I felt like a kid does when he don't want to do something he knows he's got to, and so he walks slow and does everything he can think of to put it off. But I had to do it, and here was the deputy saying, 'Well, you ought to have a fine trip,' and me thinking, 'Sure, fine trip,' and that other looking like a big beetle. He give me a—what do you call it? Helmet? Helmet and goggles, and they put 'em on me, and so there wasn't nothing to do but climb in. Jees, I wished then I'd never heard of New Haven, that I was a barber or something. So I made to climb in, see, and Joe was pushing me and my stomach felt funny, and I stopped and looked at Joe and I says: 'Take your hands off me. What you want? Wanna help me get killed?' But Joe was a good sort and so when I was in I held out my hand, thinking what a good guy Joe was after all, see, even if I didn't get back safe.

"Then the fellow climbed up where I was and started strapping a big belt around me, and I told him they wasn't no need of that, that I wasn't only not going to try to jump out but that he wasn't even big enough to throw me out. Well, he said he knowed that, that the belt was in case I fell out.

" 'Fell out?' I says.

" 'Sure,' he says, 'she might buck you out like a horse.'

"Men do funny things, don't they? Anyway, I sat there and I thought I was looking at the ground for the last time. I never was much on walking. Then he got into another seat and opened the throttle wide open. I shut my eyes and grabbed something, and I swore I was going to sit like that until we got to New Haven. We hadn't gone far when the engine slowed up again and I opened my eyes right quick and there was a house and a fence right in front of us. I couldn't even shut my eyes again.

"And then just as I thought we was going right into it we slewed around and when I got my breath again we was headed back the way we come. Then he stepped on her again and I shut my eyes and held on. And after a time when it got to what I thought was a smooth place I sneaked another look and I was right opposite the top of a tree and if I'd looked long enough I could of looked right down on top of a couple of houses. And then—but I got a weak stomach, anyways.

"Well, after a while I seen they wasn't nothing

to do but stay where I was and make the best of it. And I sure aimed to stay there as long as he did. I didn't dare turn around to see where he was, and looking out made me dizzy, and so there I was. But I learned one thing: I don't overwork my luck no more. Yes sir, ever since then I've been as easy on my luck as I could.

"If you'd ask me how it looked from up there, I couldn't tell you. I don't know. But I looked out to the side once and seen the whole ocean before I could get my eyes shut again. The ground is good enough for me.

"Anyway, after a while it felt like all my insides was falling out of me, and I shut my eyes tighter and held on. And then we bumped on the ground and after a while we stopped. Well sir, I sat in that damn thing for about ten minutes before I could move, and when I did get out it was like I had had a spell of sickness or something. We was in a big field on the edge of town, and the airplane fellow was walking about smoking a cigarette. And I lit one too, and felt a little better. I felt like taking a handful of that dirt and eating it.

"The fellow had run the airplane across the field and up close to a big cliff where you couldn't see it except you were in the field, and pretty soon here came Gus with a couple of trucks. He had been laying for us where the deputy had told him to watch out, and had followed us, see. Well, we set to work and transferred her. There was three or four fellows who come up to see what was going on, and one of 'em says 'What you got there, mister?' And Gus says right off, 'U. S. mail, brother,' and kept right on.

"Pretty soon we was through and Gus got his boys right on out with the stuff. And I took a full breath for the first time. The airplane fellow was standing around watching us, and he says:

" 'Whatcher going to do with your crate?'

" 'Crate?' I says. He waved his hand at the airplane. 'Hell,' I says, 'I ain't got no airplane. I don't never want to see one again even.'

" 'What'll you take for it?' he says. 'I might buy it back from you.'

" 'Gimme a hundred,' I says, 'and take it.'

"So he did. I was glad to get even that much back, see? All I wanted was to break even, and I figured we'd about do that, even if we never got the rest of our stuff. But I figured on doing that in a couple of days. I was like you: I called 'em hicks myself, then.

"Well, me and Gus held the thing while he started it up, and we watched him go off in it. He turned and waved his arm at us, and I waved back. 'So long,' I thinks, 'and may I never see you again.' That's what I thought then.

"All of a sudden Gus hauls a telegram out of his pocket. 'For you,' he says. 'I nearly forgot it.'

"It was from Joe and it said: 'Hold Gilman, no matter how. Coming next train.'

" 'Gilman?' I says. 'Who's Gilman?'

" 'Oh, that's the name of that J. P. that sewed us up,' Gus tells me.

" 'Hell,' I says, 'how can I hold Gilman here? Joe must be coo-coo. Hold Gilman?'

"Gus couldn't make no more out of it than me, and so we got in his car and drove on to town. And at the hotel we found one of the boys waiting in the room with a couple of bottles. They had got the stuff put away all o. k. We was all set for Joe to get back now. And then we opened a bottle."

We had been in town for some time. My friend drove skillfully while he talked.

"Well?" I prompted.

He laughed harshly. "Well is good," he said. "Do you know what was in them bottles?" I was silent, and he answered himself: "Water. Pure unadulterated water; the stuff that it rains, you know." He became again unprintable. Then he settled down once more to narration. "And every damn one of them bottles was the same. I jumped Gus right off, but he swore they was all right when he bought 'em and they wasn't no chance for anybody to tamper with 'em until they was stopped. He had opened one or two of 'em on the road.

"And then about dark Joe comes bulging in. Me and him both says 'How about it?' at the same time.

" 'Did you turn the trick?' I says.

" 'Where's Gilman?' he says quick, not answering me.

" 'What's he got to do with it?' I asks.

" 'Everything,' Joe says, looking like he was about to have a stroke.

" 'Didn't you get the stuff?' I asks, feeling my insides turning cold.

" 'How could I? The one that drove you down here had it all the time. The other one just laughed at me when I stuck him up. Called me a hick."

" 'You mean to say you ain't got that money?' I says again, trying to understand.

" 'That's exactly what I mean. But if you'll show me where Gilman is I'll damn soon have it.'

" 'Who in hell is Gilman?' I asks. 'You keep on talking about Gilman—'

" 'Didn't you get my wire?' Joe cuts in.

" 'Yeh,' I told him, 'but the only Gilman Gus and me knew was that J. P., that as far as I know is at home eating supper by now.'

" 'And you don't know who Gilman is?' Joe kind of screamed at me. His eyes were popping and his face looked like it would bust right off his shoulders. 'Gilman is the fellow that brought you down here—' " My friend the bootlegger turned a corner viciously. The pedestrian, however, escaped. " 'Him and the deputy are that judge's twin sons!' "

September 27, 1925

Yo Ho and Two Bottles of Rum

SHE WAS A SWEET THING to see, wallowing like a great enceinte sow in the long swells of the Pacific. Rolling was her habit: from side to side she went even in the calmest sea, sighing and groaning like an elephant with an eternal belly-ache, like a huge nondescript dog trying to dislodge fleas; it was said of her that she rolled even while tied up to a dock. But in heavy weather, in a sea which gave her every excuse to wallow to her heart's content, she became singularly and remarkably steady.

Her best speed was ten knots—four knots from side to side and six knots forward. Perhaps this was sufficient, perhaps more speed than this would have blown her crew overboard. A casual observer would have thought so anyway, looking down from the bridge, seeing them squatting quietly, meager and fleshless, small and naked as children; yellow wisps of men clothed modestly in shirts, still and unfathomable as mummies or idols.

Manned by Chinese, officered by the scum of the riffraff of the United Kingdom, a scum which even the catholic stomach of the dominions beyond the seas refuses at intervals, vomiting it over the face of the globe, she did her six knots, rolling and groaning her stinking way through Eastern waters from Canton to the Straits, anywhere the ingenuity of man might send a cargo. She might be seen anywhere; tied rolling heavily to a wharf in Singapore, weathering a typhoon in an anchorage known only to admiralty charts, next year in Bangkok or the Dutch Indies. Strangely enough her personnel did not change much. It was as though every soul aboard had been caught hopelessly in an inescapable dream. A dingy dream, for she was with the exception of the bridge deck and the officers' quarters filthy from stem to stern. Her personality was soiled and kind, she sailed under the British flag and years ago in Newcastle a humorist with a clairvoyant eye christened her, when she was youthful and yet undisillusioned, "Diana."

Pride is a funny thing, in the various forms it takes. The American or the Latin "goes bad" and drops out of sight, assimilates himself with people and conditions among which his destiny casts him, becomes (sentimentally perhaps) noncommittal regarding his nationality. But the

Britisher is still British, the lower he goes the more blatantly British he becomes. It was so with the officers of the *Diana*, particularly with Mr. Freddie Ayers, the mate. Perhaps the other officers had less to be British about. The captain was Welsh, his beard was like a red explosion and he spoke a tongue regarding which only one thing could be said: It was not English. It was most palpably not English. The chief engineer was Scottish. He had a face like a bitter walnut and spoke no tongue whatever. The rest of the officers with the exception of the third mate, who was Eusian [*sic*], and led or was led a dog's life in consequence, being neither one nor the other, yet having a sacred drop or two of British blood to saddle him with the white man's responsibilities while at the same time his lesser strain denied him the white man's pleasures; the rest of them seemed to have sprung blackguards full-fledged from the womb of time, being British and nothing else. The owner's agents seemed to understand the captain, however, and as it was not necessary that anyone understand the chief engineer, they got along just as well. As long as the whiskey held out, that is.

Mr. Freddie Ayers did all the talking for them. He talked all the time, waking and sleeping; he slept with his eyes open also, as a matter of precaution, perhaps. It was this, the sight of Mr. Ayers on his back, his china colored eyes gleaming dully, like a cadaver, that caused the third officer to fear him like death. But waking and in the earlier stages of his daily inebriation Mr. Ayers was the soul of joviality and wit as he sat in the saloon clasping his tumbler, sucking his straight short pipe, so palpably and blatantly British with mackerel eye and his moth-eaten Guardsman's moustache. It was he who prior to killing him through an unavoidable accident dubbed the sibilant flitting messboy "Yo Ho."

"Such a jolly name, y'know," he explained in his insufferable London voice, braying brassily in hearty appreciation at the chief engineer. "Navy fashion, hey?"

The chief gaped his toothless nut-cracker face at the first officer, replying as he did to all questions by sucking a gill of diluted whiskey into himself. And Yo Ho the messboy became, accepting the name foisted upon him without surprise, appearing on his hissing straw slippers when they bawled for him, receiving their curses, serving them efficiently and with remote yellow tolerance of the vagaries of the white man.

The Diana with a cargo of American-made sewing machines was out of Canton, bound for Bangkok, when Mr. Ayers the mate killed, through an unavoidable accident, Yo Ho the messboy.

The captain stared at Mr. Ayers morosely

across the incandescent burst of his beard. "What kill'm for?" he asked.

Mr. Ayers emptied his glass and for the nth time sought to justify himself. "I tell you it was an accident. I mistook him for the bosun. Damned stupid of me, I grant you; but damme, it's done now. I can't recall the blighter, can I, sir?" Mr. Ayers filled his glass again, viciously. "Plenty more of the fellers; one Chinee like another."

The chief engineer here spoke amazingly, supporting the mate. "Do wi'oot," he mumbled. Then quite clearly: "Rrrotten lad." Mr. Ayers and the captain looked at him quickly and he retired modestly into his glass, taking a mouthful, and sat chewing it mildly.

"But what kill'm for?" the captain repeated.

"Dammit, sir," Mr. Ayers said with justifiable exasperation, "ain't I a white man? Can't I kill a native if I want to? I ain't the first man that ever did it, any more than I'm the first man that ever made a mistake. I never meant to do the chap in; it was the bosun I was looking for. He had no business popping out on me so suddenly, before I had time to recognize him. His own bloody fault."

The bosun, having got accustomed to being knocked about by Mr. Ayers, had developed his powers of resistance to where a blow with a bit of wood, such as had done for the luckless Yo Ho, did not faze him at all; he assimilated it as he did labor or typhoons or any other inexplicable act of Fate. But Yo Ho's young and comparatively untried skull was thin and when Mr. Ayers, suffering a mild indigestion, was informed after dinner that a party shifting cargo in the after hold had gone forward to mess and left the hatches off, he knew a red rage. Yo Ho responded in swift alarm to his bellowing and scurried forward after the bosun.

The more Mr. Ayers thought about his stomach and the unclosed hold the madder he got, so taking his short, heavy stick which he humorously called the bosun's wife, he tramped furiously after Yo Ho's fading shape.

The tropical stars swung overhead, swinging slowly about the Diana's masthead; the deck was dark. This was Mr. Ayers' excuse, this was why he felled the first man who appeared in the fo'c's'le doorway. Only this happened to be Yo Ho flitting back to the saloon, where he knew he would be in demand by this time. And thereby hangs a tale, as the fiction writers say.

"So, you see, I couldn't help it," Mr. Ayers reiterated. "I wasn't after him. Fool should have kept clear, or announced himself. You can't blame me for keeping discipline aboard ship, y'know."

The captain only grunted. He combed his beard awhile. "Bury'm soon, mister," he said at last.

"Righto, sir," Mr. Ayers agreed, breathing easier. He raised his voice: "Yo—" He paused sheepishly, recovering himself, remembering.

The chief engineer regarded him with malevolent pleasure. "Ye'll aye fetch yerr ain whusky the noo, mon," he croaked.

And tomorrow brought its own troubles. While Mr. Ayers was making arrangements to bury the messboy at sea a deputation from the fo'c's'le waited on him. They were quite calm about it, no fuss and feathers, too calm in fact. Yo Ho must be buried properly on land. Mr. Ayers tried his usual method of storming and cursing them down, he tried logic, then cajolery. But they were unshaken, and Mr. Ayers, looking at their calm, inscrutable faces, saw something there that gave him to pause. There is something eternal in the East, something resilient and yet rocklike, against which the Westerner's brief thunder, his passionate, efficient methods, are as wind. Yo Ho must be interred in earth. There it ended. Or did it end there? Mr. Ayers, coarsened, surfeited with undisputed domination, with his bland conviction regarding his racial superiority; Mr. Ayers looked from face to quiet face, remote and expressionless as so many idols, and Mr. Ayers felt something cold somewhere within him. He took his problem to the captain.

The captain knew his East. His only reply was to curse Mr. Ayers, the dead messboy, the sea and the entire fabric of a civilization that invented ships and sent men to sea in them, in his native Welsh.

"We'll have to do something soon," Mr. Ayers added, strangely humbled. "He won't keep long in this latitude."

The captain, his beard more explosive than ever, cursed Mr. Ayers again in Welsh. After awhile Mr. Ayers, chastened and silent, followed him to the bridge.

Thus it happened that a ship carrying a valuable cargo, a ship of twelve thousand tons requiring thirty-nine men to operate her, must change course and run three days for land in order to put ashore one dead Chinaman. And it bade fair to become a race in very truth, for, as Mr. Ayers said, in these latitudes near the line. . . .

Mr. Ayers' chastening lasted overnight. He bolstered his integrity, sharpened his white man's superiority with whisky, and the next morning he blustered out on deck, trying so hard to be his usual self that he over-did it. But against that wall of contemplative Oriental calm, of pre-occupation with something far, far older than Mr. Ayers and his mushroom civilization of a short yesterday, he knew again a sense of irritating inferiority and uncertainty. And all the time Yo Ho lay forward under a spread tarpaulin on the fo'c's'le head, ignoring them all. He didn't care what Mr. Ayers thought about it. Mr. Ayers repaired to the saloon and had a whisky-and-soda.

The Diana rolled and wallowed on. Days burned slowly, terrifically overhead; night followed with no diminution of heat. Mr. Ayers lurked sweating and cursing in his cabin, counting the hours until they could get rid of the body, until the ship became again a sane world for a man to inhabit. He'd not have thought doing up a native would make a man this jumpy, but Yo Ho seemed to have become a part of him: he was Yo Ho alive, Yo Ho was himself dead on the fo'c's'le, laughing at himself. Soon Yo Ho became more than a dream of Mr. Ayers', and by the captain's order they moved him aft to the poop deck. These latitudes under the equator, you know. . . .

The ship sailed on, Yo Ho slept with his fathers in his own celestial glory; and one night Mr. Ayers, blackguard though he was, went to the rail and hurled the stick which he humorously called the bosun's wife far, far into the darkness. The ship sailed on.

They raised land at last, and just in time; an island off Cambodia point, the southmost cape of the mainland of Siam. And here again the East raised its implacability bodiless as mist against the West and civilization and discipline. They were all going ashore to put away Yo Ho. The captain contemplated his yellow, impassive crew briefly, then delegated the first and second mates to go along, and retired to his cabin swearing. The chief engineer and one of his henchmen joined the party for the sake of the outing.

There was a village. They procured a bullock and cart from the headman while numberless children, naked and shining as pennies, appeared silently as animals, staring at them without offense, as children. Yo Ho's cousins and friends loaded him into the cart, putting beside him two wicker baskets; and with the four white men walking to windward and the Chinese following behind, the procession set out.

The sun was red and implacable as a furnace mouth; once the beach was behind and they were among great impenetrable trees the heat became terrific. Mr. Ayers looked back at the calm, unsweating Chinese with envy and exasperation, mopping his florid face. They followed docilely, with their eyes bent earthward, trotting, trotting. Mr. Ayers cursed and mounted the cart. If he ever got this bloody business over with! His three companions followed his example, and then the engineer's assistant made a discovery.

"Ow, look 'oo's 'ere," he exclaimed. They looked. In one of the wicker baskets was food for Yo Ho, and in the other were two bottles of whisky, to be put in his grave with him, lest he wake and hunger, or lest he be too poor to make gifts, as is desirable.

Mr. Ayers felt a qualm: he was really quite unsettled over the whole business. But they soon settled him. As the engineer, breaking again into rare speech, put it: "Wull ye rob me o' ma ain bairn?" stopping his walnut of a face with the bottle neck.

" 'Oo cares for a bloody nytive?" his assistant supported him, drinking in turn.

By the time the second bottle was exhausted they were all singing and shouting. The sun swung lower and hotter, and the jungle was imminent with night complete and impenetrable, like a blanket.

"We'll be needin' more whusky the nicht," the chief interrupted himself to suggest. This was an obvious truth, and they ceased singing to stare at one another.

"Ow, that's orlright," the engineer's satellite assured them, "Freddie's the lad to get whisky for 'is pals, 'ay Bucky?"

"Hell," said Mr. Ayers, "how am I to get whisky in this place?" He looked about at the jungle, and at the narrow slashed pathway. Behind them the Chinese trotted tirelessly.

"Why, 'ow'd you get this?" Mr. Ayers focussed his eyes, staring. "Done in a Chinee, didn't yer?"

Of course. It was quite clear. And there were —Mr. Ayers looked back again—literally thousands of them, trotting, trotting tirelessly.

"I say," said Mr. Ayers suddenly, "pull up a

bit, will you? I'll run back and kill another Chinee; get some more whisky," he explained, leaping to the ground.

"Ho, we'll all kill one," the second mate amended. "Get plenty while we're at it."

They sprang from the cart. The Chinese stopped as suddenly and stood huddled.

"Careful, now," Mr. Ayers hissed for caution. "Don't frighten 'em; might put 'em up a tree, y'know."

The Chinese stood watching them as with simulated carelessness the white men approached them. Then the engineer's assistant, doubtless having his sporting blood up, sprang suddenly forward with a blood-curdling shout. The other three sprang after him, but too late. The quarry had faded into the trees, silently as a mist. But the pursuers were undaunted. The engineer's henchman howled "Gorn aw'y!" and plunged bellowing after them, and the four whites in the lust of pursuit stumbled and fell and rose again, whooping and shouting through the undergrowth, while ever and anon the assistant engineer's "Gorn aw'y!" rose vainly against the silence of jungle ten thousand years old. But not a Chinese did they find. The quarry had melted away like so many shadows.

Darkness had already fallen when one by one they straggled back to the road. They also drew closer together, hushing their breathing and their voices as the tropic night dropped suddenly as a curtain and great hot tars burst soundlessly almost at their finger tps. Intoxication had gone completely out of them.

They struck matches and examined the road. No tracks: the cart must be between them and the beach. They retraced their way, walking swiftly, following the slashed path in the treetops overhead. One stumbled occasionally and rose cursing, running to join the party again, knowing the hushed terror of nothingness. When at last (after how many hours they knew not) they saw a faint light, they were almost running. It was the village; then they heard surf and saw the pale luminousness of the sea, and the lights of the Diana in slow oscillation.

Something loomed suddenly before them; it was the cart, with the bullock placidly ruminant in the shafts. Mr. Ayers shouted and the bosun's voice in quiet reproof said: "Aw li', Mlissy" from somewhere near his feet. Mr. Ayers struck a match.

The crew squatted placidly about in the dust, courteously waiting the white man's pleasure. The bosun rose and his men followed suit silently as bats.

"Mlissy no come, no go boat," the bosun explained. "Mlissy come now, aw li' go boat."

Mr. Ayers struck another match and looked into the cart, uselessly, for the cart was empty.